DAISY C
DAYS

Also in this sequence:

1. Daisy Chain War
2. Bread and Sugar
3. Daisy Chain Dream

Joan O'Neill

Daisy Chain Days

*Hodder
Children's
Books*

a division of Hodder Headline Limited

Dedication

This book is dedicated with love to my daughters, Elizabeth and Laura, my friends and mentors, and all my family who bring me joy, and in memory of Daisy, our beloved and faithful golden retriever, who we miss so much.

Text copyright © 2004 Joan O'Neill

First published in Great Britain in 2004
by Hodder Children's Books

The right of Joan O'Neill to be identified as the Author of
the Work has been asserted by her in accordance with
the Copyright, Designs and Patents Act 1988.

10 9 8 7 6 5 4 3 2

A Catalogue record for this book is available from
the British Library

ISBN 0 340 88178 X

Typeset in Bembo by Avon DataSet Ltd,
Bidford-on-Avon, Warwickshire

Printed and bound in Great Britain by
Bookmarque Ltd, Croydon, Surrey

The paper and board used in this paperback by Hodder Children's
Books are natural recyclable products made from wood grown in
sustainable forests. The manufacturing processes conform to the
environmental regulations of the country of origin.

Hodder Children's Books
A Division of Hodder Headline Limited
338 Euston Road
London NW1 3BH

Acknowledgements

With warmest thanks to Emily Thomas for her expert knowledge and editing skills, and for her interest in my work from the start, and to all at Hodder Children's Books who asked for more.

I'm especially grateful to Jonathan Lloyd, for his unfailing support, and Keirsten Clark, and all the team at Curtis Brown, for their attention to detail.

Thanks to Mary King for reading the ms, and her contribution in terms of sharing her specialised knowledge of Refugees with me; Pat Keane for his practical advice; Jenny Bolger for her interest and conversations about refugees; June Flanagan for her insights, and Mary Markham for her interesting comments.

I'm deeply grateful to my Writers Group: Julie Parsons, Sheila Barrett, Alison Dye, Phil McCarthy, Cecilia McGovern, and Renata Aherns-Kramer for their patience, criticism and vision.

I'd like to thank all my family for their enormous encouragement; to Elizabeth and Laura for editorial comments, and Robert for his computer skills in times of crisis.

Most of all thank you to all my readers who wanted to know what happened next.

I'd like to thank all my family for their enormous encouragement; to Elizabeth and Laura for editorial comments, and Robert for his computer skills in times of crisis.

Most of all thank you to all my readers who wanted to know what happened next.

To a Squirrel at Kyle – Na – No

Come play with me;
Why should you run,
Through the shaking tree
As though I'd a gun
To strike you dead?
When all I would do
Is to scratch your head
And let you go.
W. B. Yeats

1

It was a brilliant Sunday afternoon in September, one of the last remaining days of summer. The garden shimmered in the heat. Apple and pear trees groaned with fruit. Drunken bees droned around them. Butterflies flitted among the lavender and roses. All was peaceful now that Dad had stormed off.

The sun filtered through the twists and tangles of branches and glossy green leaves of my poplar tree at the bottom of the garden. I sat in its centre curled up on an old rug I had nicked from our six-year-old golden retriever Trudy's basket.

Streaks of sunlight poured through the branches, trickling warmth as my Biro scrabbled across the page. The rough bark scratched my skin through my top. This was my hiding place, where I came to write in my diary. Under its green-leafed canopy the trailing branches widened out to form a dark, rounded dome.

Ivy covered its trunk and brambles grew untamed along the boundary wall. No one ever came down here except John, the gardener, to dump the weeds, rousing me if I fell asleep. I often wondered what it would be like to fall out of the tree in my sleep, crack my head against the trunk. I imagined the crimson blood pouring down the trunk, the sudden limpness, and Mum's screams when I was finally discovered unconscious on the grass. I always did have a lively imagination.

This was my private place; not even Rebecca (Becky), my older sister, knew about it. But then she was hardly ever around these days. We used to spend our summers together playing tennis, and swimming. All that changed when she went to Trinity College to study medicine last year. She changed. I miss her not being here as much to tease me and laugh with me about boys. Only this lunchtime I heard Dad complain to her, 'I never see you these days.'

Becky had stared into the distance. 'I'm busy,' was all she said, and turned away.

'You should be here sometimes with your mother,' he'd said.

'Isn't that your job?' she'd retorted, storming off leaving Dad and me staring after her.

She'd been very grumpy lately. I don't know what's the matter with her. Now that she was a college student, she seemed a lot older and she didn't confide in me so much.

Mum and Dad seemed to do nothing but argue lately too. Mum complained about how late Dad had got home the previous night. He said that he'd met some important people and had got held up. They hardly noticed me sitting there while they sniped at each other. I grabbed an apple and shifted away from the row that was brewing, escaping down here where I sat still until the fluttering in my heart stopped. When at last I heard the sound of the front door bang and Dad's car drive off to his afternoon surgery everything inside me quietened down enough for me to take out my diary from its plastic folder.

Recently I had become an expert at making myself invisible, because I hate rows. Dad and Mum had been at each other's throats, acting as if they hate each other. Why does it have to be like that? Being the teenager in the family. I should have been the one throwing the tantrums. That's what's expected of teenagers. Yet, I'm the quiet one, the peacemaker, which is a waste of time. I might as well be as moody as the rest of them for all the difference it makes.

Why do they make me feel so bad? I wrote in my diary. What did I care? I had my best friend Sarah Shaw, who lived across the road, and whom I'd known all my life, and my other best friend, Kim O'Driscoll from school. We share all our secrets, go on crazy diets together, discuss spots, exchange beauty secrets. Sarah envied me my thick, straight hair but it was mousy compared to Becky's shining mane, and utterly lifeless. I'd been dying to get highlights but Mum refused to let me. She said the sun would bleach it, but so far it hadn't and the summer was almost over.

We talked about boys a lot too. Boys would be Sarah's only topic of conversation if she had her way, but I couldn't understand what she sees in the boys she fancied. Last summer I had a crush on Scott Brady, who lives on the corner of our street. I'd known him since I was eight years old. We'd played together as children. He was always joking around, never taking anything seriously, much to his parents' exasperation sometimes. He didn't seem to notice me much. Perhaps he only had eyes for cars. I really liked him but he was out of my range. It was hard at the time, but my feelings soon faded and, besides, he was too old for me. At seventeen he was studying for his leaving certificate. As Sarah and Kim pointed out, he wouldn't take any notice of a fourteen-year-old. Still, I wondered what it would be like to have a real boyfriend of my very own and for a second I felt lonely.

Up in my tree I snoozed, only woken by my mobile ringing. It was Sarah.

'Hi, want to go for a walk?' she asked.

'Okay. I'll be over in a few minutes.'

She laughed and clicked off.

Mum was standing on the patio in front of her easel, painting. She was lost in concentration, unaware of being watched. Her hair was a fiery halo of gold around her pretty, oval face, her unruly curls diffuse in the light. In her cut-off shorts, and her smock hanging loosely from her shoulders, she looked like a girl — much younger than forty, anyway. Then she looked at her watch, and turned quickly to go back inside. I waited until she had gone before making my own way up the garden path to the house. But Mum stepped out before I got to the back door, holding a glass of water.

'Oh, there you are,' she said.

The sun struck the cut-glass prisms as she lifted the water to her lips, throwing a myriad of coloured light across her face and giving her a theatrical expression.

'I like that,' I said, examining the soft pink roses on her canvas.

'It's a mess,' she grumbled, gazing at it critically.

'You say that about everything you paint, but you know it isn't.'

'I have such a headache,' she sighed, taking another gulp of water. 'I'll never get everything finished in time for the exhibition.'

'Shall I get you an Anadin?' I asked.

'No thanks, love.'

'Wear your sun hat then.'

Her chaotic curls shook negatively. 'No, I'm almost finished.'

She picked up her brush and continued painting. Trudy, lying on her side, one eye open protectively, grunted contentedly.

'I'm going over to Sarah's,' I said. 'I won't be long.'

Trudy's ears immediately picked up. I put her on her lead and we went across the road to Sarah's house.

Sarah was stretched out on a sunbed in her garden, her sandals kicked off, her head thrown back, her baseball hat at a precarious angle on her head. Her skin was golden, the freckles across her nose like a dusting of fine brown sugar.

'There's nothing to do,' she said, moving restlessly, her face blank, a sure sign that she was bored. She wasn't the only one who thought that hanging around the house was boring. So did I, but I still hated the thought that the summer was nearly over and we were going back to school the following day.

'I can't believe we're back to school tomorrow,' I said sadly.

'I can't wait,' she said. 'Fifth year is a doss, no exams so we can have a laugh. Can't hack this hanging around, it's such a massive waste of time. I'm dying to see who's new this year.' Her eyes glazed over.

She meant the boys of course.

During the summer Sarah had become boy-crazy, obsessed with having a boyfriend – and always going for the 'wrong type' too. Previous summers we'd spent all our time in each other's houses playing games, dressing up, or messing with make-up. These days I had to go looking for her if I wanted to spend time with her.

Trudy was eyeing me, anxious to get going.

We walked along the East Pier, Sarah wiggling her hips exaggeratedly. The pier was crowded with Sunday strollers. Children were playing on the green opposite

Teddy's ice-cream kiosk. I liked it here. As a child I had often played around the bandstand, and the rocks behind the wall, while Mum sat and chatted with her friends. Sarah and I bought ice creams, and sat side by side on benches overlooking the harbour, watching the HSS ferry drawing away from the jetty. Magnificent boats lined the marina; music blared from one of them. Things were looking up for Dun Laoghaire. It was a more prosperous place these days.

On the way home we stopped at the café. Seated on the terrace was Becky with a dark-eyed boy I'd never seen before. They were drinking cappuccinos. She was laughing at something he said. Laughing her loud laugh, her blonde hair cascading down her back, she looked as if she hadn't a care in the world. For a moment I considered going over to say hello to her then decided against it.

'I'm thirsty, let's have a latte,' Sarah said, her eyes on the waiter.

As soon as we sat down her mobile rang. Sarah then spent several minutes chatting, reorganising her social life, twisting her hair or fiddling with her bracelets. She was obviously talking to a boy. I ordered two cappuccinos then I turned my attention to my sister, wondering where her boyfriend, Simon, was.

Becky and I used to be great friends, talking about clothes and boys and all kinds of things. But she'd lost interest in me when she went to Trinity and started dating Simon Caulder. She'd grown away from me and I was sad about that. Now as I watched her animated face, heard her tinkling laughter, I wondered if she was disenchanted with Simon and his ideals.

Tall and confident, with long legs, straight blonde hair and big blue eyes, she was a real beauty in the same oval-faced way that Mum was, and had the boys drooling over her. She looked stunning even in scruffy jeans and a baggy sweater tied around her waist. Simon, a second-year politics student, had a confident air and inquisitive mind. He was a member of the Green Party and had encouraged Becky to be politically aware, including her in all the party's activities. She was an asset to him because she was intelligent and pretty and interested in everyone – except for her own family it seemed. Sometimes she and Simon were like an old married couple, bickering all the time. But Becky was the boss in that relationship – or so I'd always thought – with Simon putting up with her nagging good-humouredly.

Sarah, her eyes glittering as she clicked off her mobile, said, 'We'll want to be at school before assembly.'

'Why? We never go in early.'

'I want to see Ryan.' She struggled to keep her excitement at bay.

Ryan was the school bigmouth. I loathed him.

'You see him all the time,' I protested.

'Only in a crowd.'

I raised my eyes to heaven.

8

On my way home I rounded the corner and walked smack into Scott Brady, tinkering with his car. His handsome face was pinched with nervous energy. There was a sheen of perspiration on his brow. Scott was waiting to start a mechanical engineering degree course at University College Dublin once he got the exam results he needed.

'Hi Beth!' he called out.

I stopped.

'How's it going?' he asked, wiping his grimy hands on a clean rag.

'Fine. How are you?'

'Living it up as you can see,' he laughed.

His eyes shone a wicked blue, and he had a mischievous grin. He was popular with everyone. I hadn't seen much of him lately; he'd been working as a lifeguard down on the seafront.

'How's tricks?' he asked. 'Like my new set of wheels?'

'Nice,' I said, admiring the sleek, second-hand cabriolet VW. 'When did you get it?'

'A few days ago. Traded in Matilda, she'd had it. It's a pre-results pressie,' he said, making a big deal out of it.

Scott loved cars. He spent what little spare time he had tinkering with either his or his father's.

'I hope you get the results you need,' I said.

He raised an eyebrow. 'I hope so too or there'll be killings. The parents are giving me grief. Mum's worried sick, she says she's having a terrible summer. Dad's insisting on getting me career advice in case I don't get the 475 points I need. I should have got out of here, gone to Croatia with the lads, but there you go.'

'Well . . . Good luck,' I said, and whistled for Trudy.

'Thanks. Where are you rushing off to?' He grinned at me, pushed his tangled hair out of his eyes.

I could feel myself blushing. 'Home. School starts tomorrow. I have to sort out my uniform and books.'

'I know, you can't wait to get there.'

I made a face and Scott laughed. 'Like to come for a drive, test the engine?' he said.

I looked at Trudy.

'She can come too.'

Trudy looked at me beseechingly, her tail wagging.

'Okay – why not,' I said.

'Come on then.'

Scott squeezed Trudy into the back seat and we got in. He started the engine, and with a confident shift of gears we were off, sweeping round corners, driving along the seafront, my hair whipping around my face in the wind.

'What do you think?' Scott called out.

'Good!' I shouted to make myself heard above the roar of the wind.

We swung right to Dalkey and the Vico Road.

'Nervous!' he called out as he sped up Killiney Hill.

'Of course not!' I lied, trying to soothe Trudy, who was cowering in a corner. 'But what if the cops are out on speed checks?'

'Don't worry, we're not going that fast. I've no intention of killing you,' he said, laughing.

The wind blew my hair everywhere; Led Zeppelin blared out from the CD player. Lights studded the bay. Stars were appearing in the darkening sky. Scott drove home slowly, and I savoured the magical scene. He pulled up into his driveway.

Trudy leapt out and stood waiting anxiously for me on the path, wagging her tail with relief. I sat still for a moment, my head still woozy from the gushing air.

'Thanks,' I said, getting out.

'You weren't scared, were you?' he laughed.

'Only of the cops catching you.'

Scott's eyes shone with amusement. 'You look terrific these days, Beth, all tanned and glowing.'

'Thanks.'

Trudy was pulling on her leash.

'I'd better go,' I said. 'Thanks for the ride!'

'Pleasure,' said Scott. 'See you around then.'

'Yeah!'

I shut the front door with relief. I still felt a bit awkward around Scott, even though I didn't fancy him any more.

The house was quiet. I went into the kitchen.

Becky was there, her eyes red rimmed from crying.

'What's the matter?' I asked her.

'Nothing, I'm fine,' she said quickly, turning away from me.

When she turned back she put on a cheerful smile and I decided not to probe her too much.

'Were you out?' I asked.

'Pub.'

She crossed to the fridge, got out a carton of milk, slopped it into a glass.

'I was looking for you,' she said. 'I wanted to say sorry for shouting at you earlier on.' She spoke with exaggerated slowness to keep her voice steady. She'd had a few drinks.

'That's okay, I went for a drive with Scott.'

'Oh! And what happened?'

'Nothing. He took me for a drive in his new car.'

'He fancies you,' she said confidentially, moving closer.

'No he doesn't.' I made a face. 'I'm only a kid in his eyes.'

'Beth, you're fifteen going on sixteen and grown up for your age. You can tell a mile off Scott fancies you. He's finally noticed that you're not a kid any more.'

'Rubbish!' I was embarrassed.

'Did he . . . you know?'

'What?'

She pursed her lips and blew me a gushy kiss.

'No he didn't.' I was annoyed.

'No need to take that tone. I was only asking – anyway, Scott's a nice boy.'

'I don't fancy him,' I insisted – not sure whether that was the truth or not.

'You used to . . .' Becky reared. 'I know lots of girls who do.'

'Good luck to them.'

'What is it with you? Is my little sister playing hard to get?' She laughed at me over the top of her glass.

I looked away irritably, wanting to tell her to mind her own business but not having the nerve. 'Give it a rest. I'm not in the mood.'

She sighed. 'You're right. You're better off without a boyfriend. I've had it up to here with Simon . . .' She sat looking into space.

'Why? What's the matter?'

She suddenly looked crestfallen as she said, 'He's like the rest of them, can't be trusted.'

'What! Has he been seeing someone else?'

She drained her glass. 'I think so.'

'Do you want to talk about it? I'm good at keeping secrets, especially if it has anything to do with that fit boy I saw you with in the café,' I said, moving closer to her, dying for her to confide in me.

She looked up sharply.

'He's nice, who is he?' I coaxed.

'That was Luke, a friend from college. We had a few drinks, nothing more.' She sighed. 'Not like Simon. He takes his friendships a bit further.' She took a deep breath.

'Anything I can do to help?'

She shook her head. 'I have to sort things out for myself. Don't tell the folks!'

'Of course I won't.' I looked at her. 'I like it when we have little chats. I've missed that.'

She grinned. 'Yeah, me too,' she said, but her mind was somewhere else as she stood up.

In my bedroom I stared into the mirror of my dressing-table gnawing my lip, full of doubts as I thought about what Becky had said about Scott fancying me. I didn't believe her. I studied my reflection; my skin glowed in the light from the bedside lamp, and my eyes sparkled, but my hair was flat and mousy. I wished I was gorgeous and blonde, like Becky, or I had Mum's curls. Anything but this dead straight, boring hair of mine.

In bed I wondered whether Becky was having real problems with Simon or if they were just imagined. I'd heard him accusing her before of being possessive. I sat staring out of the window, looking at the harbour lights wishing I were grown up and not a helpless schoolgirl.

'*Sometimes it feels like everything is out of my control,*' I wrote in my diary, feeling miserable about the following day and sorry for Becky.

Becky says there are lots of things we can do to get some of the control back, ways to make our voices heard. Something simple like wearing a T-shirt that tells people you're a peace protestor. She spent a lot of time on the Internet getting her point across – www.petitionon line.com. She had designed her own petition and found loads of like-minded people to sign it. Now she was busy forwarding the signatures to the relevant government agencies. She was also in touch with the Stop the War Coalition and the Campaign for Nuclear Disarmament, and in the process of composing a thought-provoking letter to the leader of the Green Party to help organise a peaceful protest in our area. Knowledge is power, she'd said.

I heard Dad coming in. Though he was a pain it was comforting to know that he was home early and that there wouldn't be another scene in the morning with Mum shouting and him banging out of the house. What's the matter with them anyway? I thought. Why can't Dad be more supportive of her? Why can't Mum curb her temper, for our sakes if nothing else? They know we can't stand their stupid rows that always end with Mum in floods of tears and Dad reminding her that a doctor's hours are twenty-four seven and she knew that when she married him.

His surgery, in the town centre, has become extremely busy recently with the population explosion. He holds evening clinics on Tuesdays and Thursdays, and plays golf at weekends when he can manage it. Mum is resentful, being on her own so much. I couldn't blame her, but I hoped they were going to be all right.

2

Sarah and I turned in through the gates of Mary of Hope. A former convent school, now a comprehensive, we walked straight into Ryan Godfrey swaggering up the drive. The son of Jim Godfrey, a wealthy local businessman and TD (MP) for Dun Laoghaire, he was captain of the Junior school rugby team, winner of the cross-country running championships, head of the debating society, an all-rounder, and a bully in my view. He was a year ahead of us, a senior now, and in none of our classes except drama, for which I was grateful because there were always rumours circulating about him, and his friends, none of them good. Sarah fancied him like mad. I couldn't see what she saw in him. He was good-looking in a haughty way, with high cheekbones, big blue eyes and thick blond hair that flopped over one eye, but he was also nasty. I would sooner have gnawed off my knees than allow him to touch me.

She sidled up to him. 'Hi Ryan,' she simpered.

'Oh – Sarah!' he said, casually, looking her up and down.

He glanced at me. 'Hi Beth,' he said in an unfriendly tone, his blue eyes icy-cold.

Ryan moved out to go past us, walking rapidly, Sarah hopping along beside him trying to keep up, and grinning like a Cheshire cat, asking him questions to keep his attention. I lagged a few steps behind, furious with her for following him. It was cringe-making. She had spent the previous year chasing him, slobbering up to him, trying to get him to 'go out' with her, and he hardly noticed her.

We all parted at the main entrance, Ryan going off to join his friends, a glint in his eyes.

'He's so gorgeous, don't you think?' Sarah said wistfully as we went up the stairs.

'No! He's a total jerk.'

'He's my dream man,' she insisted with a smug smile that indicated that she could get him if she wanted him.

Typical of Sarah! She was my best friend and I loved her but she had this irritating way of thinking that she was so beautiful that she could get any boy she wanted.

'Beth, you're not listening, are you?'

'No.' I walked along the corridor ahead of her.

'Beth, why are you acting like this? You're not jealous, are you?'

I stopped and stared at her. 'Give us a break! You know I can't stand Ryan Godfrey.'

'Well I like him. Is that so terrible!'

I didn't like her tone. 'Well, if you insist on chasing weirdos who treat you like dirt . . .' I stomped off, furious with her for starting a row on our first day back.

I slumped down into my chair in our cold, antiseptic-smelling classroom with its old scarred desks. At least the blackboard was clean, and the oak floor freshly polished.

I picked out a desk next to a window, hoping Kim would arrive soon. Sarah took the desk next to mine. I stared out of the window. Kim O'Driscoll, our other best friend, arrived and sat the other side of me. Kim was a keen student, and usually top of the class. It was the first time ever that we'd got to school before her. Her dark eyes gleamed with pleasure at the sight of us.

'Howya!' she smiled.

Kim was always bubbly, even at school.

'What's up with the pair of you?'

'Nothing!' we chorused, looking in opposite directions.

'Did you get to see Ryan?' I heard her ask Sarah under her breath.

'Yes, we had a long chat this morning!' Sarah exaggerated.

I rolled my eyes.

Sarah caught me. 'It's true, we did.'

'Okay. I believe you!' Kim said, laughing.

'He's so gorgeous,' Sarah said.

'Sshh, here's Mr Higgins,' Kim said.

Mr Higgins, our English teacher as well as the Head Teacher, strode in, a pile of books under his arm. His glasses perched on the end of his nose. The rest of the class trailed in, some discussing the latest film they'd seen, others moaning about being back at school.

'Good morning boys and girls,' he said, his steely blue eyes scrutinised the class.

'Good morning Mr Higgins,' we chanted, flatly.

'I hope you had a good summer.'

'Yes thank you,' some said, the rest of us didn't bother to reply.

'Don't suppose any of you are ready to settle down to some work.' His voice was full of cheerful regalia but his eyes seemed to regard us with distaste.

'No, Mr Higgins,' someone said.

Everyone laughed.

Mr Higgins banged his desk. 'I must insist that you settle down,' he said, a warning undertone in his voice.

By mid-morning it was as though we'd never been away. We were back to the grindstone with the same old teachers parading in and out of the same old classrooms. The lunch hour was spent outdoors, playing tennis. Ryan, and his friends, Goofer Keegan and Spider Conroy, arrived Ryan and Goofer condescended to give us a game. I didn't enjoy it because of the way they sliced the ball and sent it spinning at an alarming rate, either to show off or annoy us. Eventually, on the pretext of searching for a lost ball, Kim and I abandoned the game and went off to sunbathe at the far end of the playing field. We were not particularly athletic anyway.

The others joined us. Sarah made a production out of sucking up to Ryan, supplying him with chocolate I'd swear she'd bought specially for him, and offering him her last cigarette. She was posing and pouting, getting into his good books by taking his side when anyone dared to argue with him. By the end of the afternoon I was exhausted from watching her.

Wednesday was officially our half-day, but there was optional drama class, our favourite, so we stayed on.

Mr Potter, or Potty as he was affectionately nicknamed, our speech and drama teacher, was already there, poised and alert, his greying hair neatly brushed back from his elfin face. At least *he* was pleased to see us again.

'Hello everyone,' he greeted us with enthusiasm as we signed in and took our places.

Goofer sat beside Sarah.

'You can't sit there,' she said.

'Why?'

'I'm keeping this place for someone else.'

Ryan sailed past. Sarah's face flamed with embarrassment. Goofer sniggered. 'Are you sure?' he asked her nastily.

Potty cleared his throat to get our attention. 'This term I thought you might like to do a musical. What do you say?' he said, looking round at us all.

There was an enthusiastic chorus of 'Oh, yes please!' from the group.

'*West Side Story* is the one I've chosen. The music is by Leonard Bernstein, the lyrics by Stephen Sondheim. It is based on a book by Arthur Laurents. For those of you who are not familiar with this story it transfers Shakespeare's *Romeo and Juliet* to nineteen-fifties New York. The love story of Romeo and Juliet becomes that of Maria and Tony. The feud between the houses of the Capulets and the Montagues is recreated in one involving two teenage gangs, the Jets and the Sharks. The famous balcony scene is reenacted on the fire escape of an ugly New York tenement.' Potty's hands gesticulated as he spoke.

All this information was greeted with great enthusiasm.

'We'll start the auditions for the principal parts of Maria and Tony next week.

'You'd be a terrific Tony,' Sarah simpered to Ryan, flicking her hair in a sickening gesture.

'Thanks,' he said.

'I wonder who'll get the part of Maria?' someone said. Sarah preened even more.

Everyone was talking all at once, paying no attention, when there was a knock on the door.

'Come in,' Potty said.

The door opened just a crack.

'Don't be shy,' Potty added. We all stared at the slowly opening door.

Then a boy appeared in the hall. He was tall, with broad shoulders, olive skin, luminous black eyes and a mop of curly dark hair. He stood there, elegant in a navy army jacket and faded jeans, his bag slung over his shoulder.

'May I help you?' Potty asked with a theatrical upsweep of his eyebrows.

The boy stepped forward. All watched with interest, the girls staring at him admiringly, the boys eyeing him suspiciously. His skin glowed; a loop earring hung from one of his ears. He was incredibly good-looking, with perfectly shaped features and an exotic quality. He wasn't from round here, that was certain.

'My name is Alexandru,' he said, in an accented voice. 'I'd like to join the Dramatic Society.' He enunciated each word carefully, then waited, his face alert, his gleaming eyes questioning, his head tilted to one side.

Potty looked him up and down. 'I haven't seen you before. You're new to this school?' he asked.

'Yes,' the boy said.

'Can you sing?' Potty asked, aware of the tension the boy's presence had created.

'Yes, Sir.'

Potty trained his sharp blue eyes on him. 'If you're keen then this is the place for you. But we're just about finished for today,' Potty said, glancing at his watch. 'I'll fill you all in next week.'

As we were leaving Ryan walked up to Alexandru. With a glint in his eyes, and wearing the smug smile that

Sarah and most other girls found irresistible, he stopped Alexandru in his tracks.

'What did you say your name was?' He smiled charmingly, pretending to be friendly.

Alexandru looked at him. 'Alexandru.'

'Alex*andru*!' Ryan repeated, emphasising the 'dru'. He leaned over him, saying with a big mocking grin, 'So you're new to these parts.'

'Yes.' Alexandru's voice was calm, but his body language was tense and his eyes were dark.

Ryan lifted his haughty face. Not bothering to introduce himself he studied the boy. 'Where are you from?'

'Bosnia.'

Others turned. Sidelong glances were thrown in Alexandru's direction.

Ryan smiled unpleasantly. 'What are you doing here?'

Alexandru ran his fingers through his hair. 'Escaping the oppression in my country.'

Ryan leant towards him and, still smiling, asked in a confidential tone, 'Is your da a diplomat or something?' knowing darn well that he wasn't.

I knew from experience that his cool charm was deceptive. It hid a cruel streak in Ryan Godfrey.

Everyone laughed as if this was a fantastic joke. Sarah laughed the loudest. She was stupid.

Alexandru winced. 'No.'

'How long have you been in this country?'

'Three years.'

Potty, on his way out, stopped and looked solemnly from Ryan to Alexandru. 'Everything all right?'

'Yes, Sir,' Ryan said, quickly stepping back.

Potty hurried off, a satisfied smile on his face.

Ryan continued to fire questions at Alexandru like he was Immigration, or something. Alexandru, not sure whether or not his interest stemmed from anything more than curiosity, answered each one. It took only a few minutes for Ryan to extract everything he wanted to know.

Though he'd never laid eyes on him before it was obvious from his look that Ryan didn't like Alexandru. He was a threat.

'Come on lads, move your asses, let's get out of here,' Ryan said, throwing Alexandru a backward glance.

They strolled out laughing, bellowing to one another, banging the door behind them. Seething, I watched them go, listening to their voices reverberating down the corridor. Alexandru stayed rooted to the spot, staring after them.

Uneasily I edged up to him, reached out and touched his arm. 'Hi, I'm Beth.' I held out my hand.

He looked at me then clasped it and shook it firmly. 'Hello,' he said.

'I'm sorry they were so rude just now.'

He ran his hand, trembling a little, through his hair. 'It happens,' he said.

'Take no notice of Ryan. He thinks he can say and do whatever he likes.' I stopped short, seeing his unease. 'I can't imagine being in a strange country where you don't know anyone.'

He looked at me with clear, grave eyes. 'It's tough but I'm getting used to it,' he said.

There was a strained silence.

'Have you ever been in a musical before?'

'No, I haven't.'

'Neither have I.'

I hesitated; my attempts at conversation were agonising. My mind went blank. I dug my hands into the pockets of my new blazer as we left the classroom. Sarah was walking ahead.

To my great relief Mademoiselle Du Blanc, the French teacher, passed us by.

'Bonjour!' She smiled at us.

'Have you met Alexandru, Mademoiselle, he's new?' I introduced them.

'*Alors!*' She shook hands with him. 'I shall see you in my class, n'est-ce pas?'

'Yes,' Alexandru said and left with a polite 'goodbye'.

'That Ryan Godfrey has a nerve, what was he playing at?' I said to Sarah on the way home.

She shrugged. 'He doesn't like the fact that this handsome foreigner has stepped in to queer his pitch.

'He's so cruel — and vicious — they all are.'

'You know Ryan. Likes to throw his weight around. Makes him feel important.'

Once outside the school gates she rummaged in her bag for a cigarette. 'It was inevitable,' she went on. 'Alexandru is good-looking, and he's exotic.'

She held her cigarette in her cupped hand; her iridescent blue and star-spangled fingernails glittered in the sunshine as she lit it. 'They saw this perfect specimen and wanted to damage him,' she continued, laughing at the idea of it.

'It's not funny,' I said angrily. 'They were picking on him. He was like a defenceless child. Imagine what the poor guy must think of us.'

When she saw the look on my face she laughed. 'Don't take it so seriously. It's all harmless fun.'

I wasn't so sure about that. It wasn't remotely funny. 'They weren't joking. They meant trouble,' I said.

'You're giving me a headache.' Sarah looked at me with a pained expression. She blew smoke in my face, threw her head back and walked on, making it clear the subject was closed. I went silent, withdrawing because I didn't want a row.

'Let's go down to Music City,' she said. 'Check out the talent there.'

We went down George's Street. It was busy with shoppers, and hot.

'By the way, are you still on for the disco tomorrow night?' said Sarah.

'Yeah, I suppose so,' I said unenthusiastically.

'I've nothing to wear,' said Sarah. 'I think I'll have a look for something new.'

'You've got a wardrobe stuffed with gear.'

'I'd like something new, something special. I'm tired of always wearing black.' She linked arms with me. 'Besides, you never know who might be there. I want to be looking as gorgeous as I can . . .'

I threw my eyes up to heaven, but at least we were pals again.

3

Mum's car wasn't in the drive when I got home, but our cleaner Elvie's battered one was. The house was quiet, the radio on faintly in the background, the drone of the Hoover coming from upstairs.

'I'm home,' I called up, then went into the kitchen to put the kettle on and sat down in the soft glow of the afternoon to wait for Elvie to come downstairs.

Elvie Woods was a hardworking woman. She had worked for our family for the past ten years, and she 'did' for Granny, too, and another family who lived up the road. On Saturdays she worked in a supermarket. Most of her earnings were spent on her three children. 'Compo money' she called it, short for compensation for the fact that they were fatherless. Not that it was her fault. He died from alcoholic poisoning soon after Sammy, her youngest son, aged twelve, was born. Though she referred to her deceased partner, Mick, as her husband, rumour had it that they'd never actually been married.

'Wouldn't you think they'd put things back in their

places when they finished with them?' she was muttering as she came into the kitchen.

She stood in the doorway, a rainbow of colour in a purple top and red tracksuit bottoms. Her face was plastered in make-up, her magenta hair held back with a fluorescent hair band.

'Howya!' she said, sashaying into the room, her heavy body sagging with the weight of the black sack she was carrying, her cheeks flushed pink from exertion, her earrings swinging.

'Those bedrooms were a nightmare. I haven't even done Becky's yet. She won't come out.'

Elvie liked to work with empty rooms.

'She's home?'

'Yeah she is, and sulkin' over somethin'. The hours she wastes while I'm slavin' trying to keep yis all clean.'

'She's probably studying.'

Elvie looked at me. 'Whatever it is she's in a right mood this time.'

'What's new? A hot cuppa?' I suggested.

She checked the clock. 'Lovely, that'd soothe me nerves.'

I put the kettle on to boil.

'School all right?' Elvie asked, grabbing her red plastic handbag from the counter, taking out her cigarettes and matches.

'Just about,' I said cheerily. 'There's a new boy in the sixth year. He's Bosnian. Joined the drama group. Ryan Godfrey and his gang were really hostile towards him.'

'Oh, Ryan. What happened exactly?' Elvie dragged on her cigarette.

'Ryan plagued him with questions, gave him a hard time.'

I didn't want to be too specific for fear that Elvie would relay it round the neighbourhood. Her mouth was as big as the Titanic, Mum said. But for all that she had a heart of gold, and we all loved her.

'That Ryan's a nosy so-and-so. The poor young fella is probably straight out of a refugee camp. What did the teacher say?' Elvie asked.

'Potty didn't seem to notice. Ryan kept his voice deliberately low.'

'Cute shaver that Ryan Godfrey. He should show a bit of charity to the less fortunate instead of swaggering around the place as if he's Christ's first cousin. Boy's wha'!' Elvie exclaimed.

'Well his name is *God*frey,' I said.

She laughed. 'They think they own the world.'

The boiling kettle screamed like a hyena, jolting me with fright.

'Make it strong so you could stand on it,' Elvie said.

I put three tea bags in the pot, let it draw, and poured it out in a better mood, comforted by Elvie's no-nonsense remarks.

'That's grand. Nothing like a brew to make you think straight,' she said, savouring it.

Coldplay suddenly blared out from upstairs, assaulting Elvie's ears. She threw her eyes up to the ceiling.

'That sound's enough to scramble your brain. Why can't she play something that has a tune to it?'

I giggled and went into the hall, yelling up at Becky to turn her stereo down. The music blared louder. The front door opened. Mum came in with the shopping.

'There you are.' Elvie was on her feet twirling towards the sink, her half-finished cup of tea in her hand. 'You're home early.'

'Hello Elvie, Beth,' Mum said in a tired voice, easing the bags of groceries on to the floor.

'I was just getting down to brass tacks.' What Elvie meant was that she was about to organize her jobs in order of importance. The first thing to grab her attention was the wilting bowl of flowers on the dresser. She lifted them out of their vase and dumped them into the sink.

'I'm not touching that vase,' she said, looking at the precious Waterford cut crystal.

'I'll wash it, don't worry,' Mum said.

'Did you get diet yoghurt?' I asked Mum, helping her to unpack the bags.

'Yes, and half-fat cheese . . . low-fat butter. It's all there.'

'I personally don't go in for all that crap,' sniffed Elvie, shaking out her duster with the flourish of a magician taking a rabbit out of a hat. 'It doesn't make a blind bit of difference what you eat, it's all down to the genes. Look at me, I starved meself to death for months, went to them

31

aerobic classes, and that, and I still ended up puttin' on weigh'.'

Mum sighed. Elvie moved swiftly, snaking her duster round the television, turning it in circles, snapping at Trudy as she bent over the television. A bee droned behind the blind. She lunged at it with her duster, whacking it. It fell on to its back, its tiny wings rotating frantically in protest.

'Bloody bees,' she swore, whacking it again. 'Gotcha!' she said triumphantly.

The blind creaked. A spatter appeared on the window-pane.

Mum went upstairs. I could hear her call to Becky, 'It's too loud at this hour of the day,' and Becky shouting, 'Fine, Mother,' and slamming her door.

Mum came back down ten minutes later. She was wearing her painting smock, and her flip-flops. Her legs looked a little swollen in the heat.

'Are you all right?' I asked.

She shook her head. 'No one in this house ever considers anyone else! That's the problem. Why can't we have normal conversations instead of arguments all the time?'

'Same in my place, a bloody selfish lot *they* are too,' Elvie said judiciously.

As she started up the Hoover Trudy leapt up, head cocked. As Elvie quickened her pace Trudy dashed for the door in a swish of fear, her feet skittering across the parquet floor. Snatches of *Say You Love Me* escaped from Elvie's lips. She moved out to the hall, her voice croaking as it strained to reach the high notes.

I went upstairs and knocked on Becky's door.

'What'd you want?' came the sullen reply.

'Elvie wants to clean your room.'

'I'll do it myself,' Becky said.

'Why are you in such a fouler?'

There was no answer.

Elvie called up to me, 'Leave it, Beth, there'll only be a row. I'll give it a good going over next time.'

We found out what had been bothering Becky when she came and apologized for being rude. She and Simon had had a huge row.

'I broke up with him,' she said.

I stared at her. 'Oh no, why?'

'He went out with some Spanish girl, said he had to show her the sights. Didn't think I'd find out.'

'Maybe it's for the best . . .' Mum said carefully. 'Simon takes life too scrious.'

'He doesn't take me serious enough,' Becky said.

Elvie's jaw dropped. 'It seems such a waste, all the time you spent together. He's a nice chap. Helped me with the forms for the new housing scheme.

'Yes, well . . .' Mum said.

Becky looked as if she was about to cry. 'I told him never to darken my door again,' she said dramatically.

'He'll be back,' Elvie said. 'You won't get rid of him that easy.'

I left them talking and went to have a shower and change into my jeans and a T-shirt. I felt better after that. It was only a quarter to five. I got out my books, but as soon as I opened the notes Potty had given us on *West Side Story* I thought about Alexandru again and the unpleasant incident in drama. I opened my diary and wrote in the day's events. I sat deep in thought, gazing out of the window, watching the evening sky change from blue to a hazy turquoise and thinking of Alexandru. I wondered how he would fare at Mary of Hope, and I found myself looking forward to school next day, hoping I'd bump into him.

I didn't see Alexandru the next day or the day after that and nobody mentioned the incident at drama. It seemed to have been forgotten. On Wednesday evening Dad was going to be late home so I decided to go to Granny's to practise for my next piano lesson.

My granny, Lizzie Scanlon, lived in the next street to us, at number nine Victoria Terrace. With its ornamental railings and geometric-shaped gardens, the large Victorian house was tall and elegant. It had neatly trimmed hedges along either side and had been in the family since my great-grandparents, Bill and Gertie, purchased it in 1920 for six hundred pounds. Granny grew up there, had slid down the same banisters I had slid down, played hide-

and-seek like I'd done. She'd run from room to room, hiding in the huge wardrobes, or behind the shutters. Her parents passed on the grandfather clock in the hall, and the silver and crystal and porcelain to her. The basement was large enough to house a small family.

The coach house at the end of the garden opens out on to the back lane. Once upon a time it had housed two horses, and accommodated a caretaker and his family overhead. It was there that the family had huddled together during the civil war, hiding from the Black and Tans, because Bill was a member of Sinn Fein. The Black and Tans were recruited by the British government as reinforcements for the police to impose British rule. They tore around the country, plundering, looting and terrorising.

The entrance hall was bright and welcoming and smelt of flowers and polish. Apart from the colour schemes, Granny Lizzie had it looking much the same as it did in the days of her childhood. The sitting-room had been refurbished in cream and green and had the original gilt mirror over the marble fireplace, a crystal chandelier and Granny's piano.

There was a glass-fronted bookcase in the living room where Granny kept her favourite books. That's where I'd spent most of my time when I was younger, reading or being read to by her. She would sit in her black leather chair, by the fire, on winter evenings and read to me when my homework was done. Sometimes we would browse through her photograph albums, with me perched on the arm of her chair. That's how she had revealed her childhood to me, unveiling scene by scene events that had taken place in these very rooms.

Starting with her childhood snaps she would bring the mysterious photos to life. They seemed far more interesting than the idealized version of Mum's recollections. I never tired of looking at them. It was in her store of memories that they began to appear in real shapes, and became known to me. She would tell me stories of her family, many times over, her eyes fixed on the flames, her voice filled with reminiscence. She would be full of fun; almost girlish as she recalled the 'good old days', telling of parties and christenings.

Granny had been a nurse in England during World War Two. She told of bombings and of sinking ships, and of the neutrality that cushioned Ireland from the devastation that bubbled up in Europe and beyond. Granny's recollections of those days were distinct and in sharp focus.

There was a large photograph of her parents on their wedding day, their smiles happy and charming; one of Great-Auntie Karen, her sister, her hair swept up in a roll, her son John, my second cousin, on her knee spluttering with laughter. There was Karen's husband, Paul, handsome and serious in his air force uniform, confidence in his expressive, clear blue eyes. There was one of John on a rug blowing kisses, one of him in his cowboy outfit when he was about ten years old, and Vicky, Granny's first cousin, tall and dark, laughing into the camera. There were several photographs of Granny and Vicky with their arms around one another's waists, their own beloved Gran, thin and frail, a feather in her hat like a wing shooting heavenwards, standing proudly beside them.

The second album contained photographs of Granny Lizzie's twins: Eamon and Fergal, my uncles, beautiful babies with white-blond hair and blue eyes, laughing uproariously at something.

'They were delicate, but perfect too,' she would say, lovingly holding the album to her, examining it proudly. 'I was so lucky having them so soon after . . .' Her voice would trail away, her smile fade. A faraway look would appear in her eyes, and a tear, as she thought of her firstborn, a baby girl, Mary, who had been stillborn. It had been a great blow to Granny and Granddad, and had left a sadness that lingered even after the twins were born a year later. Two years after that my mum, Grace, was born, named after Grace Kelly, Granny's favourite film star. She was Granny and Grandad's pride and joy. Dad often said that they had spoilt her rotten.

In their wedding photograph – Grandad smiling gravely, his arm around Granny, serene in her white wedding dress that looked like a ball gown, her veil billowing around her.

'Your grandad had all the girls chasing after him,'

Granny often said with a roguish smile, as she looked warmly at a photograph of the slender, handsome young man in a British Army uniform. She had been a shy, watchful, serious child, she told me. This worked to her advantage when it came to recording family events. She would go off into absorbing stories about whatever she happened to be reminded of at the time. Her tales enchanted me. The long gap between the years narrowed; I was on familiar territory, the characters so well known to me that I could slip back in time in this beautiful house and know everyone in it and almost see each event.

There was Karen and Paul's wedding; John blowing out the candles on his birthday cake, holiday photographs of Uncle Mike and Auntie Peggy, their white, thatched cottage in the background, John astride a pony, happy and bewildered at the same time.

Recalling John's birth Granny would say, 'He was the best thing that ever happened to us. We were so excited – my gran stayed awake the whole of the first night Karen brought him home. He was such a beautiful baby, so good. He never cried.' Her saddest memory was of the dreadful day Paul went missing in action, Karen bursting into tears, her crying going on and on forever. Then there was the day Vicky left, her father leading her out the door and away to the wastes of Canada, their gran bursting into tears, putting out her frail hand to try and stop him.

Granny had returned home from New York, where she and Grandad had settled after the war, to take care of Bill and Gertie, who were getting old and frail. She had accepted the situation cheerfully because she adored them, and considered it her duty to look after them, and she did so without complaint, becoming their unpaid nurse, cook and companion until they died when she was in her late thirties leaving her everything they possessed.

'I was their favourite,' she would say modestly, and I would look at her radiant smile, her kind blue eyes, and could see why.

As I turned the handle on the back door of Victoria Terrace I heard footsteps, and Granny's voice calling out, 'Is that you Beth?'

She appeared, rosy cheeked and smiling, her hair soft around face. She was wearing her blue angora cardigan. Although she was well over seventy she was still glamorous, with a youthful face and a sparkle in her eyes.

'I'm glad to see you, love,' she said, kissing my cheek.

In the kitchen she said, 'Would you like a Coke or shall I make a cup of tea?'

'Coke please.'

She went to the fridge. The hand that held out the can was strong. That's what I loved about her. She was tall and strong, not like my friends' grannies, who were frail and wobbly. I sat at the kitchen table while she chopped onions and vegetables for the evening meal. She worked

39

quickly and with surprisingly dextrous hands. Her face healthy, her skin glowing.

'Tell me all your news,' she said.

She wanted to know everything, about how I was getting on at school. We chatted back and forth while she worked. She focused her kind blue eyes on me.

'You're not very happy about something?' she queried. 'Is it being back at school?'

Startled, I looked at her. She knew me so well. She came and took my hand. 'Tell me all about it,' she said, tousling my hair.

I told her about Alexandru, about what had happened at drama, how the other boys had treated him.

'It's a crying shame the way they treat the foreign youngsters who come here hoping for a better life,' she said, clicking her tongue. 'All young people are entitled to an education.'

'I just don't understand why they're so mean to him.'

She sighed. 'There are a lot of things we don't understand,' she said resignedly as she placed her casserole in the oven, then wiped down the table with a dish-cloth. 'Ireland is changing rapidly, and not for the better. Terrible crimes are being committed, too awful to think about. The refugees coming into this country are getting a very bad press,' she said. They get blamed for everything bad that happens. We're racist. We should be ashamed of ourselves for it. When you think of our history of emigration. The whole world opened its doors to us, and we went in our droves.'

I elaborated on Alexandru's good looks and sophistication. She listened intently, a smile on her face.

Grandad came in with a bag full of groceries. He was still a handsome man, agile for his age; he owned three garages in the area. Although he was officially retired, and had managers in each one, he kept an eye on them, visiting them often. He held meetings with his accountant once a week and was a shrewd businessman.

'Ah, it's Beth!' he said, giving me a hug, his eyes glittering merrily at the sight of me. 'And how are you?'

'I'm fine thanks,' I said, hugging him.

He had been a soldier in the Second World War. He was full of stories about his time in London and Germany, fascinating stories that I loved to listen to, though sometimes I had to coax him to tell them to me. He told of the bombs that fell on neutral Ireland, killing twenty-eight people and leaving two-and-a-half thousand homeless; the flying bomb attacks on London, and how brave the British people were; the D-Day landings in Normandy, and the gruelling time he spent in Germany. That was where he'd sustained his leg injury, he still walked with a slight limp as a result.

I felt myself relaxing in Granny and Granddad's company. Away from the strained atmosphere at home, this was my refuge. My safe place.

4

By the following week the daily routine was in full swing: up at the crack of dawn, the rest of the day going like clockwork with no surprises, study in my bedroom in the evenings. It was useless even to try to look for diversions because Mum or Dad would be on the warpath. Saturday had been taken up with a hockey match against Saint Catherine's, our neighbouring school, who'd trounced us, then piano practice at Granny's. Dad refused to buy a piano until he was sure I was going to take music seriously. Then on Sunday there was Mass and the boring family dinner in the evening. Even if you didn't feel like eating you had to present yourself.

On Wednesday afternoon everyone was in the Assembly Hall for the auditions, gossiping about nothing, when Alexandru walked in. He sat in the front-row chair he'd been allocated by Potty. No one spoke to him. I went over and sat next to him.

'How are you, Alexandru?'

'Fine thanks. Call me Alex – everyone does.'

'Okay.' I smiled.

Potty arrived. 'Let's get straight down to work,' he said, silencing us all. 'There is a great deal to do. No time to waste,' he continued, running a hand through his hair.

Ryan stepped forward. 'I would like to test for the part of Tony.'

Potty handed him a copy of the score and seated himself at the piano.

Ryan sang with confidence, giving it his all. But for all his physical prescence his voice wasn't strong enough to carry to the end of the hall.

'Thank you,' Potty said, motioning to Alex. 'Would you like to try it?'

Alex removed his jacket, draped it across the back of a chair and stepped forward. There were several large rips in the lining. Ryan begrudgingly handed him the score sheet. Alex held his head high and began. His reedy voice rose and soared, drowning out the sound of the piano. Potty looked up, surprised, making it clear by his expression that he recognised Alex's singing as superior.

'Promising, very promising,' he said enthusiastically. 'You're just what I'm looking for. Exactly the voice I want for Tony. With practice we can get your voice fuller, richer. Will you take the part?'

'Thank you, Sir.' Alex's eyes danced with delight.

The girls clapped, eyeing him admiringly. There was something in the air, a subtle change, imperceptible yet there.

'What about us?' Goofer said, with a shudder of rage. 'Aren't you going to test anyone else?'

'Yes, of course, if you want to have a go.' Potty waved him up.

Goofer belted out the song.

Mr Potter shook his head. 'Sorry, son, this young man is just right. I think we've found our Tony.' He cast a sidelong glance of admiration at Alexandru.

I almost felt sorry for Goofer — but only almost. He'd get over it.

'Now for Maria's part,' Potty said. 'Who would like to start?'

Sarah went up to the piano. Her voice was sweet and lovely but too weak to carry far enough.

'Beth, you have a go,' Potty urged. 'You have a good voice.'

His eyes were focused on me. I wanted the part so I could play opposite Alex, but stage fright gripped me. My voice was husky and too low. I cleared my throat and started again, cringing at the attention everyone was paying me. I did okay, but not well enough. As soon as I finished everyone started talking at once.

'Silence.' Potty's voice reverberated around the room. 'Thank you, Beth. Who'll try next?'

The other girls auditioned and all were found disappointingly inadequate.

'Ryan, you try for the part of Bernardo, the leader of the Sharks.'

'Wouldn't Alex be more suitable, being a foreigner?' Ryan asked.

'No. Here, have a go at the "Jet Song".'

So Ryan got the part of Bernardo.

Spider landed the part of Riff.

The bell rang.

'We'll start rehearsals next week. Meanwhile, I'm giving you these notes to study, and those of you who've got parts are to start practising for them.'

As soon as Potty left the hall Ryan came towards Alex. 'So you got the lead role,' he said. He looked furious. He stood facing Alex, his eyes cold.

'Congratulations,' I said warmly to Alex, who nodded appreciation.

The others stayed remote, everyone unnaturally quiet, as if something was about to happen though no one was sure what. I looked nervously at Alex, trying to convince myself that there was nothing to be scared of.

Alex made for the door, but Ryan intercepted him. I caught a sneer on Ryan's face as he looked him up and down. 'Not in a hurry, are you?'

'Yes, actually.' Alex made to brush past him.

Ryan barred his way. 'Are you one of those asylum-seekers?' he asked too loudly, making everyone start.

'No, I am a refugee,' Alex said.

Ryan was looking at Alex as though he was a freak. Stepping closer, his jaw clenched, he said quietly, 'How do we know you're not just one of them free-loading Romanian gypsies?'

'That's right,' Goofer said, sidling up.

'I am not a gypsy.' Alex replied calmly.

'Ha ha, that's what they all say,' Spider put in, slapping Alex on the back with a whack that made him jump.

There was a long, uncomfortable silence during which Alex stood bewildered. I looked nervously at him. This was familiar territory: I knew everyone here, and everyone knew me. I was trying to stay calm; everything would be all right, there was nothing to worry about. They were just teasing him, they would back off soon.

No such luck. Ryan was smiling suddenly, grabbing Alex's shoulder. 'We must have a get-together, talk about wherever it is you come from,' he said, in a mock-friendly manner.

Tersely Alex pushed his hand away, and fumbled with his bag of books, anxiety in his sweat-slicked face.

'Yeah!' said Goofer. 'That should be a bit of fun.'

To everyone's relief Ryan and his sidekicks headed for the door. Bored, for the moment at least.

That evening I headed for the sea-front, Trudy sniffing the air delightedly, pulling on her lead every time a bird flew within her range. I stopped when we reached Sandycove. The little beach was deserted. There were the footprints of birds all over it. I let Trudy off her lead. She darted around, chasing a flock of gulls barking madly. They flew off in all directions.

The sea was calm, the white frilly waves rippling on to the shore. To the left the rocks loomed dark and dangerously slippery with seaweed; waves swirled around them. A chill breeze rose. I shivered, lifted my face and breathed in the cool air. It felt good. I called Trudy. She came rushing towards me.

We walked off to the far side of the point, past James Joyce's Tower, and followed the path along the grass verge. Birds flitted around; Trudy strained on her lead, eager to go after them. We continued until we reached the curve of the bay. There I saw a lone figure in the distance. I stopped, screwed my eyes up against the glare of the setting sun and stared so hard that my eyes stung.

It was Alex!

He was standing at the edge of the grassy bank, calmly looking out over the sea; a camera grasped tightly in his hands; his sleeves rolled up. I drew closer. There wasn't a sound. I went towards him, cursing the fact that I was still wearing my stupid school uniform with the skirt that was too long.

'Alex! Hi!' I called to him.

He turned. 'Hello,' he called out, with a brief incline of his head, his voice floating back to me on the wind, his eyes grave as he turned back to concentrate on his photography.

Silent, reflective, he stared ahead. The wind ruffled his

hair and billowed out his T-shirt. Everything about him seemed elusive, mysterious, yet his gaze was clear and focused as if the only care he had in the world was to get his photographs taken. He seemed in total control. There was no indication that he'd been humiliated in any way by anyone.

'Nice evening,' I said.

'Beautiful.' He tilted his head so that his hair fell back from his face as he smiled a brilliantly white-toothed smile.

I liked his voice. I liked the way the whites of his eyes shone as he looked at me, and the way the wind ruffled his hair. I so wanted that smile to be just for me, but he wasn't even looking in my direction. He'd caught sight of a heron and was snapping away again.

I moved closer. 'What kind of camera is it?'

'Olympus,' he said, holding it out proudly. 'It's second hand. Cost me all my savings from my summer job. Left me broke, but it's worth it.'

'You like photography?'

'It's my passion. I'm going to study photography, and photograph the world. You live around here?'

'Yes. Do you?'

'A little way over there.' He glanced in the direction of the house to our left, then checked his camera.

'Nice,' I said admiringly.

'I like it.' He had the open, naïve gaze of a child as he looked over the sea and the deserted beach.

'Do you come down to the beach a lot?' I asked.

'Yes, I like to photograph the sea in all weathers,' he said.

I struggled to think of something else to say. 'Don't you ever get bored with all the standing around?'

He laughed. 'No, never.'

He shifted his weight, and settled comfortably, nothing but the rhythm of the waves and the screech of the gulls to distract him. I could feel his concentration, and his peculiar alertness. He was totally absorbed in what he was doing. Suddenly a spray of water spurted up from the sea. He jumped back, and swore in his own language. He wiped his camera, then steadied himself as he deftly clicked away again, unperturbed, unhesitating.

He turned the camera on me, taking me unawares. 'Gotya,' he laughed.

'You don't want a picture of me,' I said, embarrassed.

He threw back his head and laughed gleefully.

'I'd better go, leave you to it,' I said after a couple of minutes.

He shook his head. 'You can keep me company if you like.'

The setting sun blazed a ribbon of gold on the water, and cast a long shadow over the point.

We walked along. The air was damp; seagulls were wheeling about, squawking hysterically and flapping their wings in a frenzy of motion, gathering together as the night drew in. I watched their antics while Alexandru snapped them. The stragglers bobbed on the sea, the waves scattering them. Alex was fascinated.

Suddenly I said, 'I'm sorry about what happened to you in class.' I desperately wanted him to know that I was on his side, and that I didn't want to be associated with Ryan and the others.

'It wasn't your fault. You didn't do anything.'

'I feel bad about them though.'

'It doesn't matter. I'm getting used to it.'

I looked at him. 'But that's awful.'

He smiled, no sense of injury in his tone as he said, 'That's life.' He looked away. 'I'm not a gypsy you know, I am a medical refugee from Bosnia, I was brought here by the Red Cross three years ago.'

'Weren't you sad to leave your home?'

'No, because it was dangerous and it was full of military and paramilitary groups. When we were rounded up I escaped, and hid in the woods just like an animal. I was found by the Red Cross, and taken to a camp where it was safe. It was hard because I was separated from the rest of my family. I was on a list to go to the US, Germany or Ireland. I chose here.'

'Why?'

'Because it seemed the most welcoming, and the Red Cross officials said they'd try to find my brother and my mother and send them here as soon as possible. It would be easier to unite us if I were here rather than the US, they said. But I've been moved around quite a bit and I am still waiting for the rest of my family to join me. Then we can get a home of our own. I can't go back home to Bosnia because our house has been burnt down.'

He suddenly looked forlorn, his sadness evident in his eyes, no attempt on his part to hide it. I felt awkward, as if I'd intruded on his world.

The wind blew my hair across my face. Alex reached out and gently tucked the straying strands behind my ears. We stood there, two feet apart, not saying anything.

'It's not so bad, Beth,' he said, seeing the expression on my face. 'I can't change things but I can make the best of them. On the boat here I was scared, on my own, not knowing what Ireland would be like. That was really scary.' His voice held a wistful note. 'Then I got here and the people were so friendly and nice. There were banners in the streets with placards saying 'Welcome', everyone saying 'God bless you'. I did not speak English at the time and couldn't understand what they were saying so I was determined to learn the language as quickly as I could. I joined the English Language Training Scheme, talked to anyone who would listen to me in very bad English. I spent hours studying, reading about Ireland. Now I'm learning computers, doing a Software Localization course.'

'You've done really well.'

'Thank you. Everyone knew what we had been

through so they did their best to make us feel at home. I like the centre; everyone is so nice.

'But school . . . the boys?'

He shrugged. 'There's a good and bad side to everything. The good thing is that the school accepted me, my relationship with the boys I'll have to work at.' He looked at my doubtful expression. 'I'm lucky, I can learn a lot because the teachers are good, the Irish Government is good.'

'Aren't you homesick?'

'Of course, but if I work hard at school, learn as much as I can, I'll be able to take care of my family one day. I miss them but I think about the future all the time, and that's what keeps me going.'

'What happens if they don't manage to get here?'

'I won't stay. I shall go and find them.'

'Where will you go?'

'Who knows? It depends on where they are. I would like to go to America one day. That's why I must not fail. My family will need me to help them.'

He seemed so mature, so much older than I was, as though he'd long since accepted whatever fate had in store for him. Yet I was aware of his grief.

I shivered, drew my jacket in around me as I tried to imagine being homeless. His story had evoked an empty feeling, a feeling that I couldn't cope with. For a moment I thought of my home, Mum painting, her easel and canvases propped up against the wall in the conservatory.

Her indecision as she chose her subject, her lack of confidence in her gift. And my clever, respectable dad, a doctor who was held in such high regard, who could sort out everyone's problems, and keep their secrets. All my life I had had somebody waiting for me at home. Sometimes, I'd resented it, but I couldn't imagine being on my own, not having anybody. I felt lost at the thought. To be left all alone with nobody was unthinkable.

'Enough about me. Tell me about you . . .' Alex said, cutting into my thought.

'What do you want to know?'

'How old are you, Beth?'

The sound of my name on his lips made my heart somersault.

'Fifteen.'

'I thought you were older.'

'I'll be sixteen in December,' I added hastily. 'And you?'

'I'm seventeen.'

He looked at me seriously. His skin was so smooth, perfect like a sculpture. I stood there nervously. There was radiance in his smile that made me feel good. I smiled back. I started to say something then stopped, finding myself tongue-tied.

'It's getting cold, we'd better go home.'

He nodded. 'I'll walk back with you.' He glanced at me. 'If that's all right.'

'Of course. Trudy!' I called out.

Way in the distance Trudy stopped in her tracks, looked in my direction then ran back to me, but stood bristling when she saw Alex.

'Trudy, this is Alex,' I said, 'he's a friend.' I looked at him. 'I hope we're friends?'

He laughed. 'Of course. Hello Trudy. Nice dog,' he said, running his hand over her head.

Trudy preened herself as she circled him, her tail wagging, her eyes raised enquiringly as she sniffed the air around him. I put her lead on. We walked along the beach in silence, our trainers crunching on the stones. The seagulls were finally settled on the rocks, casting elongated shadows in front of them. Trudy loped beside us contentedly.

We turned for home, the sea-front lights twinkling in the distance. The town behind them was bleak in the twilight, the church spire rising dark against the sky. Everywhere was hushed and silent except for the musical sound of the steel wires on the boats.

'I live here.' Alex stopped outside a terraced house at the curve of the road. It was a nice, big house.'

'Have you been here long?'

'Only a few months. I was in Baltinglass but I wanted to go to a comprehensive school so they transferred me here. It's one of the few schools that does photography as a subject.'

He fell silent, and there was an awkward pause. It was a beautiful night and Alex shifted his glance to the sea and the horizon. 'Cold moon tonight,' he said, finally, then turned his gaze to me. His skin in the moonlight had taken on a silver sheen. I felt every cell in my being humming with a physical sensation that was new to me. We stood side by side and looked up at the sky; the stars were barely visible in the light of the moon.

'Why don't you come to my house for dinner?' I asked.

He frowned. 'Oh, no thanks,' he said in a rush. 'I'm expected back.'

'It'll be okay. There's only Mum and me tonight. We're having something simple like chicken . . . I'd like you to come,' I added, flushing slightly.

'I have to get back.' He looked embarrassed. 'But thanks, Beth.'

'Oh well! Some other time maybe.'

'Okay, sure . . . Bye then. See you at speech and drama.'

'Bye.'

I stood stock-still watching his dark silhouette leaping over the rocks, his hair flying back, the expression on his face as he glanced over his shoulder devoid of emotion once more. I stayed until he was out of sight. I felt an admiration for him. I also felt sad for his loneliness as Trudy and I slouched home.

The curtains were drawn in the kitchen; the smell of chicken casserole was mouth-watering.

'Have you been to Dublin and back?' Mum asked,

turning from washing dishes as I came in.

'No, I met the new boy in school, Alex, on the beach. I was talking to him. He lives in the Refugee Centre. I invited him in for dinner.'

'Really!' She wiped her hands on a tea-towel.

'He's shy. Seemed embarrassed to be asked, but I felt sorry for him.'

There was the sound of a key in the lock.

'Hello!' Dad's voice boomed from the hall.

He stood in the doorway, tall and majestic in his dark suit, his eyes heavy with fatigue.

'Well, if it isn't my better half,' Mum said sarcastically. 'Had enough of working late?'

'Got a headache,' he said, tugging at his tie, opening the top button of his shirt.

He wasn't going to get into a conversation about his work.

Mum handed him two aspirin. He washed them down with a glass of water.

'Is dinner ready?' The expression in his eyes was hard to read.

'Just about,' she said, going to the oven and taking out the casserole, slamming the door shut with her elbow.

'Smells good. I'm starving,' Dad said. 'How was school?' he asked me.

'Fine.'

'Beth invited the new boy in her class to dinner. But he was too shy to come.'

'He's a refugee.'

Dad snapped to life at the mention of that. 'Where's he from?'

'Bosnia.'

'Oh! I see. These young foreigners are cautious, probably have unfamiliar, eccentric customs and rules to abide by. How long has he been here?'

'A while, I think. He's very serious, well not serious exactly, but you know, he doesn't say much. There was trouble in school. The other boys don't seem to like him.'

'Poor kid.' Dad sat down at the table. 'There are always problems in schools between the pupils and the underdog. Not everywhere will take them. Yours is a good school, very progressive. It's wonderful that they've taken him or he mightn't have been able to go to school at all.'

'So how did he end up in this neck of the woods, I wonder?' Mum asked.

'I don't know. I know he's been moved about a lot.'

'Perfectly good reason to let him stay here then. Most of the people in our centre have been processed, and are waiting for jobs or houses. Does he have a family here with him?' Dad asked.

'No, they got misplaced along the way, but he's waiting for them to get here.'

'Must have had a terrible time in his own country,' Dad said quietly.

'Yes,' Mum agreed.

The rest of the conversation centred on the day's events,

but there was a tense, strained atmosphere. Mum and Dad seemed awkward and stiff with each other. As soon as I'd eaten, I made an excuse about having homework to do, thinking I'd leave them to talk.

'I have a test tomorrow – I really need to study for it tonight,' I explained, getting up and putting my plate in the dishwasher. 'Thanks for dinner, Mum, it was delicious.'

Upstairs I moved restlessly around my bedroom then stood at the window, gazing out over the sea black in the white moonlight. I was thinking about Alex, going over everything that he'd said to me.

5

On Saturday morning Simon arrived at the front door looking upset.

'Becky in?' he asked, stepping into the hall.

'Becky – Simon's here,' I called up the stairs.

'Tell him to go away,' she called back, loud enough for him to hear.

Simon wouldn't budge. 'I'm not going until I talk to her.'

His face was white with tension. I felt sorry for him and asked him into the kitchen to wait while I went to try and persuade her to talk to him.

'I'm not going to make it up with him.' Becky's mouth was tight with anger.

'Please come down, Becky. He won't go.'

'Who does he think he is?' she moaned, then gave in.

He was summoned to her room to be interviewed. I could hear their raised voices then silence. After half an hour, Simon emerged and stepped quickly down the stairs. The front door banged shut behind him.

Becky was standing on the landing. 'He's on his last chance,' she said. 'But we're trying to sort things out.'

Later, downstairs, Mum asked, 'Did he explain about the Spanish girl?'

'She's staying in their house. His Mum made him take her out and show her the sights,' Becky said, looking relieved.

I was glad that they'd made up. They would probably drag on for another while before the next blow-up. Their relationship seemed to be volatile, though it was obvious to me that Simon was mad about her. Becky refused to discuss him further.

Mum and I went shopping to Dublin to get away from Becky. Mum bought me a new pair of shoes, black strappy ones with clumpy heels. I love shoes. Sarah and I usually went to Top Shop for all our clothes, so when Mum offered to buy me something I wanted to go a bit more upmarket. We then walked on to HMV, where I bought the new Ms Dynamite album − feeling a bit guilty as I thought about Becky's commitment to 'world peace' and how maybe I shouldn't be spending money on myself. Later in the afternoon I sat in my tree in the garden, with my Discman and a bag of crisps for company.

I glanced up at the house. Mum was in the conservatory wiping off her brushes and screwing the tops back on her tubes of paint, tidying her work away. She looked tired and she seemed to move slowly. I sat waiting for her to stack up her easel and canvas beside all the paintings, hoping she wasn't ill or anything.

Home centred on Mum. She was the strongest influence in my life. She and I were close, whereas Becky was 'Daddy's girl'. Mum and I would sit and chat for hours. I always shared my news with her, seeking her out the moment I came home from school. I would know instantly if she were there by the atmosphere, and the comforting smell of her cooking.

But Mum had changed recently. She was a lot more snappy and often tired. She used to be fun. She and Dad used to get on brilliantly, until Dad started working harder and coming home later and later in the evenings. I'd always taken their contentment for granted until now. He didn't give her much companionship and I didn't blame her for being upset.

Dad is English. He came to Ireland to study medicine at Trinity College. Mum was a student at the National College of Art and Design. They met at a party. Dad was different to the other young men of her acquaintance, she'd often told us. He had nice manners, and he spoke with a posh accent. Not that he had a great deal to say, he was quite shy in fact. These days most of his conversation was kept for his patients. Bored and fed up, Mum threw herself back into her painting, which she'd had to ease up on since Becky and I were born.

She worked in the conservatory mostly. I liked to sit and watch her sketches take shape, then she would give them life with watercolours or oils. She painted yachts and boats, their blue and white sails flying across the canvas, their bows the colour of polished wood. She sold some of them in the local art gallery. And she took portrait commissions when she got them; children mostly, forcing them to stay calm with sweets while she captured in their emotions. Dad rarely commented on her work, though she would have liked him to. Maybe if he had done she'd have been less disgruntled with him. The place was littered with abandoned paintings, some cracked and peeling.

I shut my eyes – weary of worrying about my parents – and drifted off to sleep. I dreamt that Alex was lying beside me, his head on my shoulder, but a cold breeze woke me with a start. Shadows danced across the lawn; the sun was beginning to slip down behind a tree. The garden had faded to pale lavender. Something wriggled to the right of me. I brushed it off and put my diary carefully back in its plastic folder and hid it under the rug. Suddenly the tree seemed full of cavernous hollows, and it was growing cold. As soon as Mum left the conservatory I went in and put the kettle on to make a cup of tea.

She came downstairs wrapped in a bathrobe, her feet bare, her face half-hidden by the fall of her hair.

Dad came home early for once.

'You'll never guess who's offered to help me get more commissions,' Mum said to him.

'Who?'

'Brian Sharkey.' She grinned, looking up at him expectantly.

Brian Sharkey was a local architect, a big noise in the town, responsible for the design of the majority of the new apartments and buildings.

Dad looked up in surprise.

'He's offered to get me commissions on a regular basis for a small percentage.' Mum's eyes gleamed encouragingly at him.

Dad seemed less than enthusiastic. 'If I know Brian Sharkey he'll let you do all the work, and he'll take most of the profit.' Dad and Brian had never got on – and Mum's friendship with him didn't help.

'Couldn't you put your personal feelings for Brian aside?' she said.

'It's not personal, I just don't like the way he does business,' said Dad.

Mum and I both knew it was more than that.

Dad left the room.

'Congratulations, Mum.' I gave her a hug.

'Thanks, love.' She was studying the paint caked beneath her fingernails, a sad expression on her face. She looked like a trapped butterfly, her wings caught in Dad's power.

Granny and Grandad had a very different attitude when they heard the news about Mum's venture.

Grandad rubbed his hands together. 'You could teach that husband of yours a thing or two about business,' he said. 'He thinks it takes care of itself.'

'It will do you good, Grace, to have an interest like this,' Granny declared over tea and cakes. 'You've got to think of yourself for a change. You've been shouldering more than your share of the household responsibility recently.'

'That's part of the problem, there are too many distractions here,' Mum said. 'I'd have to get a proper studio.'

'Yes, that would be ideal,' Granny agreed.

'If I could afford it.'

'I'll ask around, see if there's anything,' said Grandad.

Grandad's friend, Barney Evans, offered Mum the rental of an unused lock-up in his old boatyard on the West Pier.

'Barney's building a new hangar so he won't need the lock-up.'

Mum was thrilled. Dad was still sulking about her plans and she'd been feeling hemmed in at home. She couldn't wait for this change of scenery. I was curious to see the place too, so I went along with Mum and Grandad to take a look.

It was a shed behind the old hangar, a secure place where parts and machinery were stored. The inside was a long, narrow space. It smelt of paint, metal and sawdust.

'Well, what do you think? There's enough space, isn't there?' Grandad asked.

'Big enough for my requirements. It's a bit dark, though,' she said.

'Once you get in new windows, get it painted and cleaned up it'll look much brighter,' Grandad agreed.

'What will it cost to fix up?' said Mum, looking concerned. 'I have some savings, but not much. There'll be new windows, plastering, painting, labour . . .' Grandad was calculating on his fingers. 'Don't worry, I'll organize all that. You keep your money for materials. You can pay me back when you're rich.' He smiled. 'Let's go and talk to Barney, I'm sure he'll be reasonable about the rent.'

'Are you sure?'

'Of course.'

'Thanks, Dad, I'll pay you back every penny.'

Pleased with themselves they went off to discuss the rent with Barney. I went to look around the yard. There were stacks of bricks, and sacks of concrete mix piled up in the old boatyard behind the shed, a concrete mixer to one side. The builders stared at me as I walked by, one whistled, one said hello. Fishermen were preparing to go out to sea.

I climbed over the wall and made my way along the narrow sea wall. A strong wind was blowing up from the sea. The air at low tide reeked of salt and the flat rocks were full of seagulls. I'd forgotten there were so many rocks and how desolate this place was. The ground was uneven. I stood and looked back at the pier, the HSS ferry standing out, stark and white against the grey buildings. From here the town looked deserted and as sleepy as a cat.

As I walked back Mum came running towards me, her face alight. 'Beth, it's mine,' she exclaimed with delight.

I hugged her.

'You'll make a fortune if you're careful, keep your wits about you,' Grandad said, coming up behind us.

He knew what he was talking about. He and Granny were comfortably off, and I'd often heard Mum say it was because he'd been so careful with money.

Dad took the news without comment. He seemed uninterested except for the financial end. 'How much is the rent?' he asked.

When Mum told him he said begrudgingly, 'If you can afford it you must be doing better than I imagined.'

He sat barely listening to her as she chatted on, but under pressure he agreed to go and look at the lock-up the following evening.

'The walls are damp, and what about that east wind? You'll never survive the winter down here. It'll be very uncomfortable,' he said when he saw it.

'I'll buy a heater,' said Mum.

Dad was annoyed with Grandad for encouraging her – he was determined to find fault.

I left them arguing and later I helped Mum pack up her art materials and canvases into Granny's old trunk.

I hated the thought of meeting Ryan and the gang on the walk to school, so I started cycling instead. I liked cycling, the wind blowing against my face, plucking through the spokes. I loved the whirring sound as I freewheeled down the hill. Sucking in my breath I raced round corners, and came to a halt with a crunch of tyres on the asphalt.

On Wednesday we went early to rehearsals. Alex was there. He was wearing a school uniform. His shirt was perfectly ironed. I had looked forward to seeing him all week, disappointed when I didn't bump into him. Rehearsals were the only chance I got to see him as he wasn't in my year. He came straight over to me.

'Beth, how are you?' he said brightly.

'Fine.' Now that he was in front of me I felt awkward in his presence. 'Learnt your lines?' I asked.

'Yes.' I saw the determination in the set of his shoulders.

'It's a great part to get.'

'The others didn't like me getting it.'

'Ignore them, they're jealous,' I said. 'They feel threatened by you.'

Alex shrugged, but he smiled gratefully at me.

'Hi Alexandru,' one of the girls called to him.

The girls were getting to know him and were treating him in a casual, comfortable manner, then Ryan came along, and any further attempts to include Alex in the conversation stopped.

Potty arrived. 'Hello everybody. Ready to start?' he greeted us.

Alex took his place on the stage. Sarah had convinced Potty to give her the part of Maria, but he wasn't happy with her performance and so most of the time was taken up with re-auditioning. Alex seemed nervous as he sang, too.

'You're not concentrating today, Alexandru,' Potty said to him. The first rehearsal hadn't got off to a very good start. Potty told everyone to try harder next time and we all left feeling demoralised.

After school Ryan was waiting for Alex again. 'You're an embarrassment,' he sneered, standing before Alex and mimicking his accent to try to provoke him.

That was the thing about Ryan. He really enjoyed goading people. It made him feel in control.

Alex was expressionless – but he stiffened. Ryan's menacing stance was sending shivers down my spine.

Then Goofer appeared, his big head nodding like a donkey, and a gleam in his eyes. 'I wanted that part, you know. I could've done a better job than you,' he told Alex.

Ryan's expression was ugly as he reached out and touched Alex's earring, took it between his thumb and forefinger, and rubbed it reflectively. 'Look at this, lads, now what kind of an earring is that?' His proximity forced Alex backwards.

Alex's eyelids twitched. He lifted his head, turned to look in the opposite direction. The hairs on the back of my neck rose. I felt a strange buzz in my head as a tinge of fear shot through me. I glanced at Alexandru. He was standing his ground, his face blank. I wanted to intervene, diffuse the situation, but I couldn't think of a way to do it that wouldn't humiliate Alex.

'Is this part of your gypsy culture?' There was mockery behind Ryan's menace.

'Yeah,' Goofer said, yanking it, making Alex's head jerk back. 'We want to know all about it. Take the damn thing off.'

Alex stayed motionless.

Ryan snorted with laughter as he yanked the earring harder, mercifully breaking it before it ripped Alex's ear.

Alex shut his eyes for a second as he withdrew from the force of the pain. A spot of blood appear at the lobe of his ear.

'Cheap rubbish.' Ryan held it up for everyone to see.

There was total silence. He had scared the daylights out of everyone.

'You are a gypsy aren't you?' Ryan persisted.

Alex continued to ignore him.

Ryan's temper flared up. 'I'll put you through that damned window if you don't answer me,' he said, giving Alex a shove.

Alex fell back into a chair.

Goofer chortled.

Suddenly Alex was on his feet again. 'I am not a gypsy,' he said, his eyes shining like ebony.

Ryan's disbelieving eyes swung away, anger bristling out of every pore of his skin. 'What do you think?' he said to the others.

Goofer just laughed, showing his buck teeth.

Spider crawled up and said to Alex, 'Why don't you go back to where you came from?'

Startled, I looked from one to the other, heat rising in my cheeks. Why was nobody stopping them? I couldn't contain myself a moment longer.

'Stop saying things like that,' I shouted.

They turned around.

Ryan started at me, breathing hard. 'Stay out of this, Beth Corrigan.'

'You should be happy now that you've hauled him over the coals. Why can't you leave him alone? My voice was rising as I looked from one mocking face to another. I stood, my hands on my hips, my mouth set in a hard, tight line.

'Will you look at the state of her,' Gillian Clifford laughed. 'Embarrassing or what?'

Fury caught in the back of my throat. 'It's not funny,' I shouted at her.

They all glared at me. Confused by their attention I blushed at their snorts of laughter, and whispers around the room.

Ryan's eyes were blue chips of glass. 'Shut the fuck up,' he said.

'Leave her alone,' Sarah intervened.

'Whose side are you on?' Ryan snapped at her.

'I'm not on any side,' she hit back furiously.

Immediately everyone stopped talking. In the eerie silence Ryan stared at Alex.

Alex's stance was uncompromising as he stared back at them, then silently he took up his bag and left. Ryan and his gang followed. Outside they stood and watched me like a bunch of hooligans as I walked past. I ignored them but I felt a knot in my stomach and fear for Alex. Now that they had had their say would they leave Alex alone? Or would they fight him? I mean, really fight him with fists and knives?

6

That evening I went up to see Granny.

'You should have seen the way Ryan and his gang spoke to Alex,' I said, telling her what had happened. 'I felt so sorry for him.'

'They won't do any real harm, I'm sure. They all come from good homes, they know right from wrong.' She looked at me. 'I worry about you, Beth. You're too sensitive for your own good. You ought not to care so much.'

'I can't help it,' I said, hurt by her attitude. 'I'm not going to let those bullies get away with it if they have a go at Alex again.'

Shaking her head, Granny said, 'You don't want trouble for yourself in school. You're a clever girl, with a promising future.'

I considered this. I wanted to be a doctor, not a GP like Dad, but a surgeon, saving lives in a developing country, or operating in a war zone, but I couldn't see how befriending Alex and sticking up for him could prevent this.

'Listen,' she said, shaking her head. 'This boy, Alex, is one of the luckier ones. He's being looked after by the state. Take the way the poor down-and-outs are sleeping rough in the shelters down at the sea-front.' She pulled her mouth sideways. It gave her face a tragic look.

'That's a weird attitude.'

'It's a safe one. Take my advice, Beth, befriend the lad but try and keep out of it – I'm sure he can look after himself.' She took both my hands between in hers, pressing them with her soft fingers.

Her hands were cool and comforting.

'So I'm to let them do what they like, get away with it.'

'There are the teachers to keep control.'

I laughed. 'Potty knew there was trouble brewing when he saw them in a circle round Alex, but he just walked out. Didn't do a thing to stop them.'

Granny was pragmatic. 'He probably didn't realize what was going on. There are police out there to enforce the law if there is trouble. There's no good you getting involved, no good at all.'

Appalled, I sat distressed and confused. This wasn't like her. She'd always believed in fighting for her principles and up to now I had taken her advice very seriously because she was sound. Suddenly she seemed cowardly; she must be getting old. Seeing my distress and confusion she said, 'Why don't you invite him to dinner on Sunday so we can all meet him, befriend him that way?'

I shook my head. 'He wouldn't come.'

'He might. Ask him.'

Later on, when Mum came home from her studio, she was clearly excited.

'The new windows are in, the plastering is done. All it needs now is a fresh coat of paint.'

'Granny thinks it would be a good idea to invite Alexandru for dinner tomorrow.'

Mum thought it was a great idea too. 'I wonder if he's handy with a paintbrush? I'd pay him. I'm sure he could use the money.'

'I've no idea,' I said. 'Ask him when he comes.'

She sat leafing through her recipe books, wondering what to cook.

'You don't have to go to that much trouble,' I said. 'He's been living here a long time.'

'I want to put him at his ease,' she said.

'I feel weird about asking him,' I said. 'I don't even know if he'll come.'

Mum went out and bought all kinds of exotic food on Saturday. It was a lovely Indian summer's evening when Trudy and I set off to find Alex. The town was quiet, shops were shuttered up, the sea-front abandoned. The summer season was well and truly over for another year. Flower boxes were still blooming, boats were lined up in the marina, yachts were moored in the deep water of the harbour, the tops of their masts tinkling in the wind. I approached the Refugee Centre, trying to get up the guts to invite him.

Alex was sitting on the steps, so at least I didn't have to knock on the door.

'Hi!' I said, throwing him an anxious look.

Trudy barrelled up to him, wagging her tail expectantly.

'Hello,' he said with a warm smile, patting Trudy on the head.

She licked his face.

'Trudy! Behave!' I said.

'She's okay,' said Alex.

'Mum and Dad would like you to come for dinner on Sunday – nothing fancy, will you come?' This was all said in one breath.

Alex smiled. 'I'd like to – thanks,' he said.

It was that easy.

'Great. See you then. I have to go to piano practice now. Come early.' I was so relieved that I yanked Trudy away and dashed off.

I told Granny the news. 'I'm so nervous,' I said.

'Don't let it show, just try and make him feel at ease,' she said.

On Saturday night I wrote in my diary, '*I'm so excited, can't wait!*' sitting in my tree, wishing I could find the words to describe my nervous state.

On Sunday morning sunlight flooded through my window. A good omen, I thought, putting on some mascara, blusher and lipgloss. I waited with fluttering heart, determined not to let anything go wrong. I saw Alex coming up the path. He looked a bit grim-faced. As soon as the bell rang I bolted for the door to be the one to let him in, Trudy in my wake.

'Hi! Found us all right, then? Come in,' I said.

His manner was stiff and awkward, but Trudy's warm, slobbering welcome put him more at ease.

'I like your home,' he said, as we came down the hall. 'You're Alexandru?' In the living-room Dad was welcoming, shaking Alex's hand warmly. 'Come through to the kitchen,' he said.

Mum was charming, too, but Alex seemed nervous and uncomfortable in their company, as if his situation here was shameful in some way. Becky appeared in her bathrobe, her hair damp after her shower. 'Hello,' she said. 'I'm Becky. You must be Alex.'

She threw herself into a chair and casually dangled her legs over the side while she talked to him. Granny and Grandad arrived and greeted him with genuine pleasure. Everyone talked at once, interrupting each other in their eagerness to make him feel at home, and, gradually, it worked.

When Mum slipped away to finish the cooking, and Grandad went out to check the garden, Granny kept the conversation going, asking Alexandru about his background – himself and his family and his life back in Bosnia. Alex really opened up to her. He told her that he was from the village of Potocari, and explained that his father had died when he was a baby and that his mother had continued to work on their farm with the help of his uncle and his brother. Alex had helped out too as soon as he was old enough. They managed well and they were happy. The Srebrenica massacre in 1995 changed their lives.

'We had to leave and go into hiding when the trouble came,' he told her. 'We got separated. I write to my mother often, but I don't hear back from her.' Suddenly his eyes were veiled, his face averted. He didn't want our pity.

'Keep writing to her,' Granny advised. 'She may get the letters. What about the Red Cross, are they working on your case?'

'Yes,' Alex told her he was hoping to have good news from them soon.

'They'll do everything to find your family and make contact with them,' Granny assured him. 'I know they were wonderful when my brother-in-law Paul went missing in action during the Second World War. They found him.'

'Yes. Don't worry, you'll have news of them soon,' Becky agreed.

'I hope so,' Alex said.

During the meal he told us about his plans for his family's future in this country. He didn't seem to think there might be any problem with them getting a house and settling down once they got here. I wanted to believe that, but the fact was that there were plenty of things that could go wrong. I knew from listening to Dad, who had refugees and asylum-seekers among his patients, that often there were discrepancies in paperwork that prevented families from being allowed to stay here. Nor was it always possible for families to be together if they did manage to stay. What if they didn't get here?

Alex caught my eye and suddenly I felt a thudding in the pit of my stomach. Then he smiled, happy and relaxed. I smiled back. Grandad broke the spell, asking if he'd like the job of painting Mum's studio. Alex said he'd be delighted with the work.

When Alex was leaving Mum said to him, 'I hope this is the first of many visits here.' And Dad wished him luck, offering to help in any way he could.

Granny saw him to the door, her arm linked through his. 'Come and visit me too,' she said, looking at him expectantly.

He promised that he would.

I walked to the gate with him, Trudy trailing after us.

'Want to go for a walk?' asked Alex.

Trudy pricked up her ears and wagged her tail in delight.

'Great.' I went and got her lead.

'It wasn't too much of an ordeal for you, was it?' I asked as we walked along.

78

'I enjoyed myself,' he said. 'I haven't really spoken much about my family to anyone since I've been here, except to you, and now your family. Talking about them was good.'

At Sandycove we explored the beach. Taking off our shoes and socks, we rolled up our jeans and waded into the water near the rocks where the gulls' nests were. My jeans got soaked.

On the way home Scott drove by and blew the horn of his car as he slowed down. Trudy raced over to him, barking her greeting.

'You'll catch your death,' he called out, laughing at the state of me.

'It's not cold,' I called back, and sneezed.

He drove off.

'Is he your boyfriend?' Alexandru asked, a light of curiosity in his dark eyes.

'Scott? Of course not!' I said indignantly.

He leaned so close to me that I thought he was going to kiss me. Instantly I moved away, wanting him to but not wanting him to at the same time. Slowly we retraced our steps to the Refugee Centre. It was getting too cold to hang around.

'See you at school, then,' I said when we reached the centre.

'Yes. Thank you for a nice day,' he said.

'You're welcome. Bye.'

'Bye.'

I walked home quickly, a wet Trudy squelching along beside me.

That night Becky slipped into my bedroom.

'So where did you two get to, then?' she asked.

'Sandycove,' I said, switching on my computer to stop a cross-examination.

'You weren't doing something you shouldn't have been doing?' she teased.

'Don't be silly, there's nothing going on between Alex and me,' I protested.

'You're very palsy,' she said, as if surprised.

'We are pals.'

'I think there's more to it than that.'

'What makes you say that?'

'From the way you look at each other.'

'You say that about every guy I come into contact with.'

'He's good-looking, and he's so polite,' she enthused, giving me a long, appraising look. 'You do fancy him, don't you? You can't tell me you're just interested in being friends with him.'

'Becky! Shut up,' I replied.

'You've gone red!' she said, laughing.

'Hey, are you sure you don't fancy him yourself,' I teased back.

'Oh, spare me,' she sighed.

She could be so maddening at times, Becky. I half-wanted to open up to her but I didn't want to discuss my feelings for Alex with anybody yet. I was too confused about how I felt, for a start, and I already felt too much for him.

'How are you and Simon getting on?' I asked, changing the subject.

'Much better. He's really behaving himself,' she said with a self-satisfied grin.

Finally she went back to her own bedroom. I got out my torch and went out to the garden to retrieve my diary from the tree, for fear Becky might find it. A pool of light from Mum and Dad's bedroom lit the garden. Mum was probably in bed, reading. Dad was out. Everywhere was silent.

I went to my bedroom to sort out my books for the next day, and fill in the day's events in my diary. I wrote about being with Alex on the beach, finishing with, '*I really like him, I think he likes me too.*'

Writing about him gave me an excited feeling. I relived the moment when he looked as though he was going to kiss me and wondered what a snog with him would be like. I couldn't wait to see him again.

In bed I lay back on my pillows, listening to Chris Martin's soulful singing. I had the weirdest feeling in my stomach. A hazy, happy feeling.

7

The following Saturday night Sarah called for me. She'd slicked back her blonde hair and gone overboard with mascara and lipgloss. She was wearing a tight T-shirt, cut-off jeans and sequinned Buffaloes. Her midriff was exposed to show off her belly-ring.

'Sexy or what?' She raised perfectly shaped eyebrows defiantly.

'Very Britney,' I said.

She looked me up and down. 'You went to a bit of trouble yourself,' she said, her eyes grudgingly admiring.

'Thanks.' I had on a new black top, with a deep V, my good jeans and my new shoes.

In my bedroom Sarah leant into the mirror, fluffing out her hair, while I painted my toenails blood red.

'Wonder if the lads will be there?' she said, pulling her mouth into a sexy pout.

She meant Ryan, of course. I hoped he wouldn't be.

Dad gave us a lift to the tennis club. It was packed. The air was hot, the music thumping. Ryan and the boys arrived and stood around. The girls from our rival school, Saint Catherine's, stood together in a group eyeing them up.

'He's here,' Sarah said gleefully.

There was something in her voice, a determination. I knew she meant business as she floated over to him going, 'Hi Ryan.'

'Hi!' he said, rolling his eyes impatiently.

'You look good,' Goofer said, leering at her.

'Thanks,' she said, laughing as she lifted her hair, and let it fall back into place.

The music grew louder. We were all on the dance-floor, dancing around in a great mass. Sarah lurched with Ryan, her eyes glowing. I looked at her. She stared back. Her eyes narrowed as she said, 'Lighten up, Beth, let yourself go.'

'Yeah. You'd better watch out, Beth, you might enjoy yourself,' Ryan sneered.

I consoled myself with the thought that the night wouldn't last forever.

A hand caught mine. I turned to see Alex standing beside me. His eyes looked luminous in the dim light.

'Hi! I said, thrilled to see him.

I looked over my shoulder, expecting to see Ryan and Sarah appear beside us with some smart remark, but they were too busy snogging. She whispered something into his ear. Next I knew they were going off somewhere. She turned and gave me an 'I always get what I want' look.

After dancing for a while Alex said, 'It's noisy. Let's get out of here.'

Outside the air was cool, the noise muffled. It was a beautiful night. A myriad of gold stars twinkled in the sky like diamonds on a blue velvet cushion.

'It's mad in there,' Alexandru said, leading me to the boundary fence that divided the tennis club from the park.

He moved close to me. His face was level with mine. His eyes were on me as he bent his head and touched my lips with his. They were soft, like the touch of a butterfly. I closed my eyes, felt his breath on my face.

'I've been wanting to do that for ages,' he said.

I couldn't think what to say.

He tilted my chin up. 'I want to do it again,' he said, wrapping his arms around me.

My heart raced and my breath was out of control as we kissed long and deep. Eventually we pulled apart.

'Where did you learn to kiss like that?' I said, breathless, touching my lips and wondering how many other girls he'd kissed before.

He laughed. 'I'm not sure it's something you learn. It comes naturally when you like somebody.'

'Really?'

'Is that so strange? You're very nice – and you're very pretty,' he said, touching my face with his forefinger.

I felt myself blushing as I looked up at the sky. The stars shone; a cloud passed over the crescent moon.

'What are you thinking?' he asked.

'I was thinking how beautiful the world seems right now.'

'You're a romantic,' he laughed, and put his arm around my waist.

I shivered, enjoying the feeling.

'Beth!' Kim's voice ripped through the air. She rushed towards me, looking panicky. 'Sarah's been sick in the toilets, I mean really sick.'

'Oh God! I'd better go.' I turned to Alex. He and I followed Kim to the loo. He waited outside until I went in with Kim, to find Sarah hunched over a toilet bowl.

'What happened to you, Sarah?' I asked her.

'I dunno . . .' she slurred.

She was green and spaced-looking.

'Let's get her outside,' I said to Kim.

We got her to her feet and dragged her outside. Alex helped Kim hold her while I phoned for a taxi.

Ryan came on the scene. He looked at Alex, his head swaying.

'What are you doing with her?' he asked.

'She's ill. We're taking her home.'

'No you're not, she's with me.' He grabbed Sarah.

Sarah's head lolled like a rag doll.

'Get away from her,' I warned Ryan. 'We're taking her home.'

Ryan ignored me. He hauled her along the path.

Alexandru followed, trying to reason with him. 'The taxi's on its way,' he said.

'Clear off,' Ryan hissed.

'Sarah!' I called to her. 'Come on, we're going home.'

She groaned and stumbled towards me. Alex grabbed her.

Ryan's hand flew through the air. The next thing I heard was his fist slamming into Alex's jaw.

Alex staggered and slumped to the ground, holding his nose.

'Jesus!' someone said.

A crowd was forming. Alex had both hands cupped over his face. When he took them away his nose was bleeding, one eye was closed and puffy.

Ryan, followed by Goofer, came after him again. I got between Ryan and Alex. 'Stop!' I screamed.

'Like you're going to make me?' Ryan sneered. 'I'm so scared.'

I didn't budge.

'Bitch!' Ryan exploded as they reeled off.

'Wankers!' I shouted after them.

The taxi drove up. We put Sarah in and got inside after her.

'Trouble?' the taxi driver said as the doors slammed.

'It's nothing,' said the white-faced Alex.

The taxi driver stopped at Sarah's house first and waited while I helped her inside. Then he dropped off Alex and me. Outside my house I turned to look at Alex. He looked awful. His eye was swollen, the corner of his lip bleeding.

'Come inside and I'll clean you up,' I said, instinctively putting out my hand to touch his arm, but he brushed it away.

'Thanks, Beth, but I'm fine. I'd better get going. I'll fix myself up at home,' he said briskly.

Suddenly, far from feeling closer to him, a gap yawned between us. The magic spell was broken.

'I'll see you around,' he said.

I woke up the next morning thinking of him and the way he'd kissed me, feeling those kisses still on my lips. Then I remembered the fight and the perfect, blissful feeling faded away.

8

Next evening I went with Trudy to the Refugee Centre. Alex appeared at the door almost as soon as I knocked.

'Hello,' he said, with a brief nod of acknowledgement. His eye was still puffy and bruised.

'Just called to see how you are,' I said.

'I'm fine.' He stood silent, looking into the distance. 'It's nothing,' he said. 'Don't worry about me. I've had run-ins before.'

'A run-in you call it! It was much worse than that. I've a good mind to report them.'

His eyes were cold as stone. 'Don't get involved, Beth.' He pushed his hair out of his eyes in a defensive gesture.

'Well, I'm your friend, you'd better get used to having me around.'

He stood frowning. 'I can manage on my own.'

'You need friends, Alex. We all do.'

He gave me a strange look. 'I have always taken care of myself.'

Stung, I said angrily, 'I didn't try and fight your battles. I was only trying to help. I won't in future!' I felt mortified, and furious at the same time. I called for Trudy and walked away. I didn't look back.

At school the next day I could see by Ryan's swagger that he was smugly triumphant. Alex was in the schoolyard; he walked over to me and said, 'Friends?'

I shrugged.

'I don't blame you for being angry with me. I shouldn't have said what I said.'

'You don't seem to want me around.'

'I'm sorry.'

I didn't want a feud between us. 'I just wanted to show them that they couldn't carry on like that.'

'I know, but really, I can take care of myself,' he said, and smiled.

I wanted to tell him that he hadn't made such a good job of it so far but I held my tongue.

He looked humble as he said. 'I do want you as a friend.'

I looked at him searchingly. 'Are you sure?'

'Sure.'

'Right, but I'm to keep my nose out,' I said, knowing that it wouldn't be easy.

'Thanks.' He smiled. 'Want to come and see your Mum's lock-up this evening when I'm finished there?' His expression was tentative.

'Sure . . .' I smiled back. 'I'll see you later.'

★ ★ ★

Trudy and I went down to see Alex's handiwork that afternoon. He came to the door, his cap at a rakish angle, his overalls paint-spattered.

The smooth white walls were dazzling and made the space look bigger and brighter. It wasn't quite finished but the place was already transformed, with new double-glazed windows replacing the old dim ones and a large sink under the window facing the sea wall.

'Wow, what a difference!' I said. 'You've done a great job.'

He shrugged. 'It was easy. All that's left is the shelves to be put up. I told your grandad I would help him.'

'Time for a break,' I said, putting the kettle on for coffee and taking the two Big Macs I'd bought on the way out of my bag.

'Special treat,' I said, handing one to Alex. We sat on the steps behind the sea wall to get away from the smell of paint.

'See these pools . . .' Alex said, pointing between the steep, smooth rocks. 'Good for catching crabs. I often fish for them down here.'

'You spend a lot of time on your own.'

'I like being on my own, I'm a loner.' Seeing the expression on my face he added, 'Not all the time. Listen, would you like to go off somewhere for the day on Saturday?'

'Where?'

He shrugged. 'Anywhere.'

'Silver Strand, it's a beautiful beach in Wicklow,' I suggested.

'Great. I'll bring the picnic.'

When we'd finished eating Alexandru looked at his watch and said he had to go.

'I'll wait for Mum,' I said. 'She'll be down soon.'

After he'd gone I washed the mugs and tidied up, then stood looking in Mum's small mirror, flicking my hair, experimenting with a new way of doing it for Saturday, pulling it back, straightening it behind my ears. It was limp and lifeless. Maybe I could have it cut in a more trendy style . . . ? I experimented with Mum's black watercolour, outlining my eyes. I applied a rose colour to my cheeks, pouting; I put it on my lips. I looked older, more sophisticated.

Suddenly, I heard the sound of loud voices. I knew for certain who it was. I kept quiet but Ryan saw me through the window and came to the open doorway. He stood affecting a nonchalant air, the collar of his leather jacket turned up.

'I saw that gypsy. What was he doing here?' he asked aggressively.

'He's working for my Mum. Not that it's any of your business,' I said, resenting his tone.

Ryan brushed past me, arrogantly, as he came inside for a closer look. I could see Spider lounged on the sea wall outside.

'Mmm,' Ryan said, unimpressed. He looked around

for a bit, then went back out to join Spider and Goofer.

'Look at you, done up like a dog's dinner,' Goofer called to me. He was sprawled out on a boulder, like a walrus. 'For lover boy, I bet.' He smacked his blubber lips in a kissing sound.

'Yeah!' Ryan sneered.

I stood in the doorway. 'I'd like you to go,' I said, looking from one to the other.

They didn't seem to hear me.

'We could have a bit of fun here, couldn't we?' Goofer glancing from Ryan to me meaningfully.

'Yeah!' Ryan said, looking me up and down.

Goofer whispered something to him. They both laughed.

I locked up and swept past them, deciding not to hang around for Mum.

Ryan's hand was suddenly on my arm, his fingers gripping my flesh, making my skin crawl. 'So, where are you off to, glamour puss?'

'Nowhere you need to know about.' I walked off.

Ryan grabbed me. 'Don't speak to me like that.' He was showing off in front of Goofer.

I wrenched my arm free. 'Ooh, I'm so scared.'

Ryan laughed, flexing his biceps, then grabbed me again.

'Ouch!' I didn't like the way he was looking at me. It made my skin crawl.

'Let her go,' Goofer said. 'Come and hang out with us,' he called after me. 'We're going to the pool hall.'

I didn't hang around. I picked up my pace, until I was running home.

Brian Sharkey was there when I got in. A middle-aged man, with a thin face. Mum was chatting to him, and making tea. She seemed to fascinate him, because he didn't take his eyes from her face for a second. I might as well not have been there.

'Brian called and I forgot all about the time, sorry love.' Mum giggled as if it were a huge joke. 'You remember Beth, Brian?'

'Indeed I do,' he said. 'My, how you've grown,' he added with a smile.

'Well, what did you think of the studio?' Mum asked me.

'Great!' I said enthusiastically. 'It looks much bigger.'

Brian asked Mum when she expected to be fully operational.

'I won't be there too much to start with. I have to let Harry get used to the idea.' Briskly she added, 'Don't worry, I'll get plenty of work done.'

'Very wise,' he said, giving her a wink – a flicker really, but I saw it.

I sneaked a look at Mum. She was sitting upright, looking very proper, but her face was bright pink.

'I warn you, I'm unstoppable when I get going, Beth will vouch for that.'

'Yes,' I said.

'I'm sure.' Brian gave her a surreptitious glance through his eyelashes. Watching them together gave me a strange, uncomfortable feeling.

Perhaps it was due to what Dad had been saying about Brian. Whatever it was, I didn't like him. I hoped that he'd leave soon, but he didn't. He sat there completely at home, an easy, assured tone in his voice as he said, 'I've every confidence in you turning out masterpieces down in that studio, Grace. My clients won't be able to get enough of your work. Isn't that right, Beth?' His tone was bantering, but his eyes were openly flirtatious.

I looked at him in semi-disgust.

'Oh, go on with you Brian.' Mum laughed with pleasure, not noticing me bristling.

At last Brian got to his feet. 'I'll get my solicitor to draw up an agreement, and send you the details,' he said.

Mum was smiling like a love-struck teenager. I'd had enough.

'Excuse me,' I said, and bolted.

Later, Mum came and found me in my room.

'You weren't very polite, rushing off like that,' she said. 'Brian's all right, you know,' she said. 'When we bought this house he was very helpful. He's a good friend.'

He was no friend of Dad's, that I knew for certain.

★ ★ ★

That evening Dad enquired how Alexandru was getting on with painting the studio.

'He's doing a great job,' I told him proudly.

Mum told Dad that Brian had called to see her.

'What did he want?' he asked gruffly.

'Just came for a chat. He has a wide knowledge of art and artists,' Mum said sheepishly.

Dad just grunted. I went to my room.

After he'd left for evening surgery, Mum said, 'He's so short-tempered lately, and he's getting worse. He doesn't tell me a word about his day or what he's doing.'

'It's because of Brian. Dad doesn't like him,' I said.

'Well, tough, he's not going to dictate who I should or shouldn't see.' She shrugged her shoulders and went to her and Dad's bedroom.

9

The following Saturday morning I told Mum and Dad that I was going to Silver Strand for the day with Sarah. I felt bad about the lie, but they would never approve of Alex and me going off to spend a whole day together on our own. Thankfully Mum was preoccupied with Becky, who had announced at breakfast that she was planning a ten-day trek in the Himalayas for 'spiritual rejuvenation' with some of her old school friends.

'With a supply of Red Bull, no doubt,' Dad had said sarcastically. It would cut in to her new term at university and Dad wasn't happy.

'Is Simon going on this trip?' Mum asked Becky.

'No, I haven't invited him,' she sniffed. 'I need time to myself.'

Dad had thrown his eyes to the ceiling.

I left them discussing Becky's plans – and her love life and went upstairs to get dressed properly. I put on my jeans and a pink top, and some subtle make-up, and tied my hair back. Dad insisted on giving me a lift to the train station on his way to the surgery. I prayed that Alex would be out of sight.

Luckily, there was no sign of him when we got there, but once Dad had gone I paced up and down nervously waiting for him. A group of boys with sports bags were standing around. They tried to get my attention by calling out to me. I kept my back to them, praying Alex would hurry up.

He left it to the last minute. Just as the train was pulling into the station, he appeared breathlessly next to me, with his camera slung over his shoulder and a small knapsack on his back.

'Did I startle you?' He laughed, having seen me nearly jump out of my skin.

'No,' I said, trying to sound casual, but feeling anxious.

Alex insisted on paying for the two return tickets. On the train we sat opposite one another. Alex leant forward on his elbow, gazing out of the window.

'I hadn't realized how beautiful the countryside is,' he said, staring admiringly across the fields as the train flew past.

The train journey was long. Other passengers looked at us curiously, making me feel uncomfortable. Alex seemed on his guard, his bag clutched tight. Once we got to Silver Strand I found my favourite spot on the beach and plonked myself down. Alex came and sat beside me. We stayed in silence for a few minutes, until he undid his backpack and pulled out a towel.

'I'm going for a swim. Want to come?' he asked.

'Okay.'

Alex dived straight in, then glided out to sea with long, smooth strokes until I couldn't see him any more. He had gone underwater. Worried, I stood up, craning for a sight of him, but he suddenly burst through the surface, closer to the shore.

'Come on, Beth, don't be scared!' he gasped, waving at me.

I changed into my swimsuit and stepped cautiously into the water. Alex was swimming towards me, blowing out his breath, while I hopped around the edge. Then I took a deep inhalation and dived in, too, coming up, shuddering, next to him.

'Not so bad, is it?' he said.

A huge wave rolled over us, lifting me off my feet. Alex grabbed me and held me against him. I could hear the beat of his pulse against my ear. I wriggled out of his grasp.

'Don't you like being held in the water?'

'No!' I swam off on my own, turned on my back and watched him swim towards me with strong, butterfly strokes that threw up sheets of water.

He caught my ankle. 'Trapped,' he teased.

I splashed him. He ducked and swam off. I floated for a while on my back, my eyes on the clear blue sky. Suddenly, I felt cold. I got out, shivering, dried myself off and dressed. Alex joined me.

'I enjoyed that,' he said, drying himself.

He got changed quickly and lay down beside me again. Propped up on one elbow he leant over me. His closeness was intoxicating. Then he lay back on the rug and drew me to him and kissed me. Time stopped, we were on a planet of our own, everything and everyone forgotten except us in each other's arms. As Alex kissed me I could feel his hands beginning to stray over my body, and I sat up. It was all going too fast. Mum and Dad had been pretty strict with me and Becky about boys, and though I knew kissing Alex was harmless, I was worried about what it would lead to, what I would want it to lead to.

Alex was looking at me, his eyes questioning. Unable to meet his compelling gaze I turned away, scared that if I stopped him now he might go off me. I felt stupid. Everyone was doing it, why shouldn't I? Yet I couldn't quite believe the logic in my own reasoning. His eyes were gazing into mine, reading the trepidation in them.

'Tell me – what is the matter?' he said.

'I don't know if I'm ready to . . .' I stopped, mortified, my heart pounding.

'We were only kissing, Beth. Don't tell me you haven't kissed a boy before?'

'Of course I have.' I didn't tell him that Ian Healy's wet sloppy lips had felt like sink plungers at the Christmas party in Sarah's house, and it had been an experience I'd had no desire to repeat. It hadn't been like this.

'You don't have to do anything you don't want to,' he said in a warm voice, but his eyes told a different story.

He was transformed back into the other formal and distant Alex, our magic moment gone. I looked at the long shadows criss-crossing the beach, biting my lip and wondering what to say and do. A breeze rose up from the sea, cooling the sun.

'You're shivering,' he said. 'Let's have our picnic or we'll be late getting back.'

He fetched his bag, laid out the picnic. There was ham, Greek salad, chicken and delicious rolls.

'Where did you get all of this?'

'Caviston's deli,' he told me proudly, almost in a motherly way.

I was impressed.

He poured coffee from a flask and smiled as he handed me a beaker. He looked pleased, watching me eat with relish. As soon as we had finished he got to his feet and held out his hand to pull me up.

'Let's go for a walk.'

We walked along the strand and sat on the wall overlooking the sea, Alex taking photographs, exhilarated by the waves, their thunderous roar contrasting with the utter silence all around us.

'The first sight I got of Ireland was from the sea,' he said. 'I thought it was so beautiful and I was so happy to be coming here.' He looked sad as he spoke.

'Will you stay, do you think?' I could feel my face go red.

'I don't know yet.' His eyes were on me, strong, compelling. 'You have lived here all your life,' he said quietly. 'You don't know what uncertainty is.'

Suddenly it felt as if everything between us was unsettled, shifting, nothing battened down.

'I'd like to escape too some day,' I said, 'see what the rest of the world is like.'

'You probably will. Come on – we'd better go. It's getting late.' He leant in and kissed me on the lips. It was a friendly kiss, nothing more.

On the way home he held my hand but his eyes were distant as he stared out of the train window. We decided to say goodbye at the station – without fixing another date. I walked home feeling confused, and as though I had spoilt things.

I let myself in the front door and went through to the kitchen, where Dad was waiting. He looked furious.

'Where were you until this hour, young lady?' he asked.

'The train broke down, we had to get a bus,' I lied, wanting to tell him the truth, tell him that I hadn't done anything to be ashamed of.

'We were anxious. You should have phoned us to let us know. That was the reason I got you a mobile phone.'

'Sorry,' was all I said, and I moved rapidly toward the stairs. I couldn't face an argument.

Becky's door was ajar as I went past and I stopped to put my head round it – she didn't seem interested in where I'd been.

'You're back,' was all she said, preoccupied with her studies.

I took a long shower, pulled my curtains and crawled into bed. As soon as I closed my eyes the day's events came flooding back. I thought of Alex, and his long lashes, the cleft in his chin, his soft skin, the way the muscles of his back moved as he swam, the musky smell of him. Would he understand my reasons for not wanting to go too far yet? Would he be patient, and if so for how long? What if I'd put him off and he didn't ask me out again?

Next morning I waited for the sound of Dad's car driving off before I went downstairs. The house was quiet, the clock ticking off the seconds as I ate my cereal. I felt strange, languid and dreamy. I couldn't stop thinking about Alex. I'd have to pull myself together. What if Sarah copped on to something, noticed that there was something different about me? I kept out of everyone's way, studying in my room.

On Monday morning I woke up late, cycled to school, swinging along the inside of the traffic as fast as I could. At the school gates I saw Alex walking just ahead of me.

'Hi there,' I called to him, getting off my bike.

He turned around. 'Beth!' he said in surprise. 'You okay?'

I nodded, all at once feeling nervous, and rushed off to class. Sarah and Kim were already there, huddled together talking and giggling.

'Hi,' I said. 'What's so funny.'

'Nothing,' Sarah said, shooting a meaningful look at Kim.

I knew that they had been talking about me. During the morning I could feel the isolation and paranoia settling in around me like a blanket. Did they know I'd gone on a date with Alex? And if so, how did they know?

I decided to sound them out at break. 'You two were acting funny earlier on,' I said. 'You were talking about me, weren't you?'

Sarah shook her head, but her eyes met mine defiantly.

'If I've done something to upset either of you I'd rather know,' I persisted.

Finally Sarah said huffily, 'You went on a sneaky date with Alex and didn't tell us.'

'How do you know?'

Sarah tapped her nose. 'We never used to keep secrets from each other.'

'I was going to tell you.'

'My house tonight then.'

Later that evening, when we were slouched on Sarah's bed, she said, 'So, why were you scared to do it?'

'I wanted to but it was like I couldn't go through with it.' Somehow I was unable to meet her eyes.

'But why?'

'I suppose I was afraid Mum and Dad would find out,' I admitted, feeling the colour rise in my face. 'But I was scared of it too. It was like I was with a stranger, and I was seeing him for the first time.'

'Not like Alex at school, but the real Alex?' Sarah said.

'Exactly.'

'Did Alex mind that you didn't . . .?' Kim asked.

'I don't know,' I said truthfully.

Sarah smirked. 'You'd better make up your mind what you want. You can't expect him to stick around and wait. He's very good-looking. There are plenty of girls who'd be willing to go all the way with him.'

That was the last thing I wanted to hear. 'I need more time,' I said.

Seeing the expression on my face Sarah said consolingly, 'It's not your fault. It's your antiquated parents who are to blame.'

Kim tittered. 'Yeah!'

'It was my first proper date. Ian Healy doesn't count,' I argued.

They both laughed at the very idea of poor Ian Healy.

'And it's not as if I'm going to settle down or anything. I have to play the field a bit first, don't I?' As an excuse it sounded lame even to me.

Kim said kindly, 'You were right to hold back. He'll respect you all the more.'

★ ★ ★

Next time I went to Granny's I confided in her about my date with Alex. I knew that she would understand.

'I'm glad you were sensible, Beth. Don't get too involved,' she warned. 'Boys like Alex are different.'

'In what way?'

'Alex is complicated. You and I both know that he has got a sad history and plans that don't include you. They don't include anyone but his family. That's all that's on his mind.'

'He'll be all right once they get here, won't he?' I said.

'What if they don't make it?' she said softly. 'He won't stay and then you'll be heartbroken.'

'We're friends no matter what,' I said, sounding more confident than I felt.

But I didn't talk about him any more, I didn't trust myself to speak for fear that the floodgates would open and the tears that were threatening would arrive.

10

Out of the blue Vicky, Granny's cousin, phoned. Her daughter Colleen was a member of the cast in a play that was about to tour Europe, Vicky told Granny. Colleen would be visiting Ireland, and planned to bring her own daughter, sixteen-year-old Tori, with her.

'I didn't know Colleen was an actress,' I said.

'She not a famous one,' Granny said.

'It's a shame Vicky's not coming too,' Grandad said, crestfallen. 'It must be four or five years since her last visit.'

'Yes, I know you have a soft spot for Vicky,' said Granny, and she laughed. 'But still, it'll be nice to see Colleen again, and meet Tori. A new friend for you, Beth.' She turned to me hopefully.

Hardly! A friend was someone you grew up with, like Sarah and Kim, not a blow-in.

'Why didn't she visit here sooner?' I asked.

'Vicky wanted to bring her last time she came, but she and Colleen had a falling out and Colleen refused to let Tori travel with her.

I knew about Tori, or course. I had always been curious about her. I'd often tried to imagine what she was like and couldn't judge from photographs and the scant information gleaned over the years. Now that she was coming to stay with us I'd see for myself. I spread the news of her imminent visit with excitement and a little apprehension.

'Pity she's not a boy,' Sarah said regretfully.

Trust Sarah to come out with that.

On the day of their arrival I wore my jeans, boots and Karen Millen top. I was anxious, wondering what Tori would think of me. Would she like me? Would we get on well together?

Grandad and I drove to the airport to meet them while Granny stayed at home to prepare a meal for everyone. As we swung up the ramp to the Arrivals car park my heart lurched with apprehension. At the barrier, while we were waiting, peering into the crowds searching the faces, I had a series of alarming thoughts. Would she fit in with our family? What if she didn't like me? What if my friends weren't cool enough? I didn't have to wait long to find out.

Grandad picked them out of the crowd.

'There you are,' he called to an elegant, willowy blonde.

'Pete!' Colleen strode towards him.

Dropping her bags and opening her arms wide, she hugged him to her large bosom. Grandad teetered on his toes, steadying himself he stepped back.

'This is Beth!' he spluttered, turning to me and then running his hand through his hair, straightening his tie.

'Beth, how lovely. I haven't seen you since you were a toddler!' Colleen said, and grabbed me to her bosom, too.

She was a pretty woman, with blonde hair caught back in a twist and blue laughing eyes, and she was younger than I imagined. A long-legged, narrow-hipped, red-haired girl stood to one side.

'Tori! Come and meet your cousin,' Colleen said and beckoned to her daughter.

We were finally face to face, but it wasn't how I thought it would be. She was lovely in a sullen sort of way, with high cheekbones, translucent skin and luscious lips.

Suddenly shy, bowled over by her looks, I said, 'Hi Tori,' in a strangled voice.

'Hi,' she drawled.

Barren green eyes met mine, looked me up and down, not a trace of a smile on her chewing-gum-snapping lips. I attributed her staring to the fact that she might be shy too. I wondered what to say next.

Grandad shook hands with her, then said with alarm to Colleen, as he took charge of their trolley full of luggage, 'I thought you said you were travelling light.'

'That's nothing! The rest is being sent on,' laughed Colleen, following him out to the car park.

Tori walked ahead of me, huddled into her jacket. I followed her.

'Did you have a good flight?' I asked, trying to be friendly.

'Terrible,' she said, tonelessly.

At the car she stood calmly, watching as Grandad and I struggled to put all the bags into the boot.

'Climb aboard,' Grandad said, endlessly good-humoured.

Colleen sat in the front. Tori and I got into the back of the car. I eyed her warily. She was staring out of the window, taut as a coiled spring, her red hair flaming in the sunshine. I wouldn't have put it past her to jump out at the next set of traffic lights. Grandad swung out into the roundabout, and on to the dual carriageway. He kept the conversation going at a furious pace to fill the awkward silence, until he was out of breath. Tori sank further into her corner. I spent the journey studying my newly acquainted cousin surreptitiously, trying to see beyond the sulky pose, wondering what she was really like behind the pout.

Granny hugged Colleen, saying how like Vicky she'd become in the intervening years. Tori squirmed when Granny hugged her next.

'Beth will show you to your room,' Granny said. 'She's going to help look after you while you're here.'

'I can take care of myself,' Tori drawled.

Back downstairs, Granny served delicious roast chicken and all the trimmings.

'What would you like to drink, girls?' asked Grandad.

'Coke for me, please,' I said.

'I'll have a glass of wine,' said Tori.

'That all right with you?' Grandad asked Colleen.

Tori eyed her mother blandly. 'She doesn't mind me drinking.'

'One glass of wine won't do any harm,' Colleen said cautiously.

Mum and Dad arrived. There was more fuss as they all greeted one another.

'What a lovely girl you're turning out to be, Tori,' Mum said.

'The image of Vicky at that age,' commented Granny.

'In more ways than one,' Grandad said under his breath.

'How do you like being in Ireland?' Mum asked.

'I'd rather be at home,' Tori said, sitting back, crossing her legs.

'Hush up,' Colleen said to her. Laughing, she added, 'When I told her she was coming here to stay she kicked up such a stink. You've no idea.'

'I didn't want to come,' Tori said insolently. 'You forced me into it.'

'It's only for a few months,' Colleen soothed, dropping a bombshell straight into Granny and Grandad's laps.

'A few months?' Granny looked aghast.

'Didn't I mention that?' Colleen smiled innocently.

'No you did not,' said Grandad.

Obviously Colleen had purposely omitted to let us know her long-term plans until she had Tori safely installed here.

'Not that we mind, we're looking forward to having Tori,' Granny said quickly, regaining her composure.

'Yes, I'm sure we'll get very attached to her,' Grandad said, eyeing Tori doubtfully.

Colleen relaxed visibly. 'Thanks, Lizzie. It means a lot to me. I knew I could depend on you both,' she gushed. Turning to Tori she said, 'You'll have a great time with Beth and all her friends.'

I could almost hear the hurry to get going in her voice as she spoke.

'Yeah.' Tori sneered, curling her lip.

I groaned inwardly and secretly hoped that Tori would refuse to stay with us.

Colleen leaned towards Granny and said, 'I wasn't happy about leaving her at home with just Martha, our maid, and Mum's not interested in looking after her,' she explained. 'Too busy with her charity work.'

Her eyes flashing, Tori said, 'You could have left me with Taylor and saved yourself the expense of bringing me here.' She was watching her mother, looking for more trouble.

Colleen spluttered, 'Don't talk nonsense.'

'Who is Taylor?' Grandad asked, puzzled.

'My boyfriend,' Tori replied, her eyes flashing. 'And I'm going back to see him as soon as I can,' she added.

The smile left Granny's face. Grandad coughed discreetly.

'Tori, eat some dinner,' he coaxed. 'You've hardly touched it.'

'I'm not hungry. Neither would any of you be if you were dragged off to the far side of the world against your will.'

'I'd feel I was going on an adventure,' he said.

'Really!' Tori raised an eyebrow at him.

'You'll have a good time with Beth,' Granny said. 'Meet all her friends . . .'

Tori threw me a contemptuous look.

'Pay no heed,' Colleen said to us, making things worse.

Conversation petered out. Nobody knew what to say. Mum and Dad hadn't said a word, dumbstruck by Tori's attitude. Tori speared a piece of chicken but didn't eat it, determined to play the victim. The rest of the meal was strained, with Tori furtively pouring herself more wine, drinking it down fast while casting sly glances at her mother every now and then, making us all feel uncomfortable.

'Home-made ice cream, anyone?' Granny asked.

'No thanks, I feel sick,' Tori groaned.

Colleen's high spirits finally deserted her. 'You'd better go to the bathroom then,' she said sharply as she focused on Tori's empty glass, her temper barely concealed.

'Beth, take her upstairs, please,' Granny said, reaching over and patting Tori's hand.

I linked arms with Tori to steady her. But as soon as I opened the bathroom door she laughed.

'I'm not sick. I just wanted to get out of there,' she said with a gleam in her eye. 'I'm not going back down either.'

She stared at me as if I was something from another planet. I led her into the bedroom. She went to sit on the bed, slipped sideways and landed on the floor.

'Are you all right?'

'Sure!'

She got to her feet, only to collapse on to the bed. Her face screwed up into a mask of self-pity as she said, 'I wanted to stay with Taylor, you know. We're so in love, we're getting engaged as soon as I get back.'

'Engaged!'

'Shh!' She put a finger to her lips. 'He's twenty-five and loaded. Wants us to have a great big wedding.'

'Wow!' I was fascinated.

I told her a little about my friends, about school. It all seemed dull in comparison to her life and she wasn't very interested.

She yawned. 'I'm tired.'

'Get some sleep, you'll feel better.'

'I guess.'

I left the room, closing the door quietly behind me.

Back downstairs Colleen was saying to Granny, 'I hate

intruding on you, Aunt Lizzie, but I didn't know what else to do.'

'Tori's most welcome to stay here for a little while,' Dad said. 'But a young impressionable girl needs her mother sometimes. What happens if she falls ill, whose shoulders will the responsibility fall on then?'

'Ours,' Grandad said gloomily.

'Tori's as strong as an ox,' Colleen said.

'She doesn't look it,' said Granny. 'Too thin if you ask me.'

'And she's very young to leave with strangers,' Mum added.

Colleen burst into tears, 'But you're family, Aunt Lizzie! I don't have anyone else since Vernon cleared off with his secretary.'

'Oh, I'm so sorry,' Granny said, going to Colleen and taking her in her arms to try to console her.

On the way home Mum said, 'That Colleen is breathtakingly selfish.'

'Always was,' Dad said. 'I'm not surprised Vernon divorced her.'

For once they seemed to agree on something.

'We'll have the responsibility of Tori too,' Dad said grimly.

I couldn't blame him. It was hard to understand how Tori had been dropped right into the middle of our family and that from now on everyone and everything would revolve around her. Weeks of having to listen to her boasting about her boyfriend loomed ahead. If I'd known she was going to be like this I wouldn't have looked forward to her coming. How would she be with my friends? I underlined the word *complicated* in my diary entry for that day when I got home, then sent a text message to Sarah: '*Come over tomorrow early, please! My cousin is here and she's weird.*' Then I settled down to a good night's sleep. I'd need it if I had to face more of the same tomorrow.

Grandad arrived with Tori and Colleen next morning. Sarah was on the doorstep five minutes later. We all sat in the living-room. I put a CD on.

'Tell me about Canada, is it anything like here?' Sarah asked Tori.

Tori raised an eyebrow. 'Hardly,' she said, a sardonic smile playing on her lips. She spotted Sarah's cigarettes.

'Let's go and have a smoke,' she said, getting up from the sofa. Sarah followed her outside, where they stood at the bottom of the garden and lit up. I stayed where I was, glad of a moment's piece and quiet.

'She's suffering from a broken heart,' Sarah said later, when we were alone. 'You've got to be patient with her, Beth. She'll be grand once she gets her bearings, and that mother of hers takes off,' she added, as though she was some kind of psychologist.

'I hope you're right,' I said. But I wasn't so sure.

Grandad drove Colleen to the airport after she'd said a

breezy goodbye to everyone and given Tori a hug, promising, 'I'll phone you often.'

'She'll settle down.' Mum tried to reassure a very worried Granny.

Granny shook her head doubtfully. 'She's a handful,' she said, 'like her grandmother.'

'She'll be all right once she gets into a routine,' said Dad.

As the days went by Granny worried about Tori staying in her bedroom all day and spending most evenings talking on her mobile to Taylor. She was sure she heard Tori crying at night, too. But Tori didn't open up to her or anybody − until she admitted to me how much she missed Taylor.

'I keep dreaming about him,' she confided. 'But I can't see his face any more. I hate it that he's so far away.'

'Poor thing,' I said, without warmth. Just then, though, I did feel sorry for her, being so far away from home.

But my sympathy soon faded when she reverted to her spoilt complaining self, while still using me as a shoulder to cry on. I grew sick of the sound of Taylor's name. She was driving me nuts with her melodrama.

'I've never come across such an antisocial girl in my life,' said Granny. 'She doesn't want to have anything to do with us. At this rate of going she'll never settle down. I don't know what else we can do for her.'

'If we're not careful I think she'll have Taylor on the doorstep before we know it,' Becky said worriedly.

Granny and Grandad were both anxious to fill the gaps Tori's parents had left, and make her happy. But Tori was clearly not a happy person by nature. How could she be with a mother who couldn't handle her and was only too eager to hand her over to someone else to be looked after? No wonder she was always so aggressive, finding everything and everyone distasteful.

I couldn't imagine what it meant to Granny and Grandad to have Tori living with them, yet Colleen had insisted that it must be them. She was so selfish that she didn't for a moment think that Tori's presence might be a burden. She took it all for granted, and so did Tori, sharing their lives without noticing what it was taking out of them. I was doing my share to help her settle down, but I was beginning to realize she never would.

11

I had expected Tori to want to spend at least some of her evenings with me, meeting my friends. But she never seemed to want to leave Granny and Grandad's. Her daily routine turned out to be different from what we had expected. She stayed in her room most of the time, like a prisoner. Even the marathon phone calls between Taylor and herself didn't cheer her up. Nothing interested her and, worse, she refused to go to school. She'd learned enough, she stated categorically, and she wanted to get a job and go out to work as soon as possible.

Granny was distraught.

'Let me have a word with her,' Dad said, as though he had some special powers.

'You can talk to her till the cows come home but she won't budge.' Granny shook her head.

'You'd better get some sense into her,' Grandad said. 'She'll be serving behind a bar before you know it.'

'Or worse,' Mum said with a worried frown.

It was Mum who finally stepped in to retrieve a

situation that was threatening to get out of control. She took Tori into the city for lunch and a bit of shopping. I don't know what she said to her or how much the bribe had cost Mum, but Tori made no protest when I called for her to come to school the following Monday morning. She was quite submissive, in fact. As soon as we arrived everyone gaped at her with curiosity.

'This is my cousin Tori,' I said to the class in general before assembly.

There was a chorus of 'Hi Tori, nice to meet you', as they greeted her warmly.

During the morning Tori sat stiff and awkward, overwhelmed more than pleased. At first she was like a sleepwalker, not entering into the spirit of things, chewing her hair, her brow furrowed, until lunchtime, when Kim, Gillian and Sarah carted her off to the canteen to ply her with questions.

'So, your mother has gone off to Europe?' Kim said.

'Is your dad not at home?' Gillian asked.

'Don't be so nosy – leave her alone!' Sarah barked, her arm defensively around Tori in a sudden proprietorial attitude.

'I don't mind people knowing that they're divorced,' Tori said sadly.

'God, you poor thing,' Gillian said with real sympathy.

'Is it really awful for you having to live with your grandparents?' Kim asked.

'The worst,' Tori said, lifting her Coke to her lips and

tilting it down her ungrateful neck, playing to at her captive audience.

'No it isn't, they're really kind looking after you,' I protested, outraged.

She glared at me.

'Will you be staying long?' Kim asked.

'Just this term. I'm going back home at Christmas. To get engaged,' she added, looking from one to the other with pride and delight.

'Wow!' Her audience was really coming to life now.

'Who is he?' said Gillian.

'What's he like?' Kim asked.

Tori beamed at them. 'Gorgeous! Think Justin Timberlake, only sexier. He's a snowboard instructor, really fit, as you can imagine. Here, see for yourselves.' She produced a photograph from her wallet. 'This is Taylor.'

He looked handsome all right, and bland.

'Where did you meet him?' Kim asked.

'He's a neighbour. I had a crush on him for years before we got together.'

You'd swear she was thirty the way she talked. While the others studied him admiringly, hooked on Tori and her stories, I shrugged and raised my eyes to heaven.

The boys arrived. Ryan introduced himself straight away.

'I've heard all about you.' Tori giggled.

'Is that right?' Ryan leered. 'Someone, get her a drink,' he called out. Almost immediately a Coke appeared.

Ryan and his mates crowded around her.

'So what's Canada like?' he asked.

Tori was like a different person now that the boys had arrived.

'Oh, it's cool,' she simpered, widening her eyes as she described the clean city, the shops, the nightlife, and good-looking men. She was the centre of attention. They were all intrigued with her.

'You interested in acting?' Ryan said.

'Sure. I study drama at my own school.'

'Can you sing?'

'Sure can.'

'You'd be great in our musical, wouldn't she lads?' he asked.

They all agreed.

'I'll give it a try,' she said, smiling sweetly.

I was furious.

On the way home I cautioned Tori about how she'd been behaving with Granny and Grandad.

'You shouldn't treat them like that,' I said.

'They're a pair of weirdos,' Tori said rudely.

I turned on her. 'How dare you say such a thing!' I shouted, anger and hurt welling up in me. 'You should be grateful to them that they took you in when you obviously had nowhere else to go.'

'Well, I'm not. I'd prefer to be at home with Taylor.'

'Will you stop going on about Taylor!' I shouted at her.

That shut her up.

'I think we should have a little welcome party for Tori,' Becky said that night.

'I'm too busy,' I scowled, wishing Tori would just go back to where she'd come from and leave us all alone.

'Doing what?' Becky asked.

'Homework for one thing.'

'And seeing Alex?'

'I haven't had a chance to speak to him since she arrived.'

It was true. I'd hardly seen Alex since our day trip and I missed him. I felt more in need of his friendship than ever. I was also concerned that his feelings for me might have changed, and that he might be avoiding me.

'You should make an effort with her, Beth,' Becky said. 'It's bad enough she's been forced to be here against her will without you being intolerant of her as well.'

I shrugged. 'Whatever,' I sighed.

As the days went by my friends warmed more and more to Tori. They would hang around talking to her in the lunch-hour, wander with us to the corner shop for Cokes and crisps. Sarah was getting very palsy with her. The two of them would go off and smoke all the time.

Their gossip sessions in the cloakroom grew longer and longer.

Tori started hanging out more often with Ryan and his cronies, too. She would sit at the back of the class perched on a desk, telling them about her world in Canada. The boys didn't only accept her, they sought her out for advice and opinion. They considered her superior – sophisticated even – just because of her accent and her 'glamorous' mother.

I was more of an observer than a participant in all of this. I would look at her beautiful, mocking face, anger welling up inside me. Just listening to her talk to them set my teeth on edge. Was this what I was going to have to put up with indefinitely?

At rehearsals the following Wednesday Tori auditioned for the part of Maria. When the music started she straightened up, and holding her head high she sang 'Somewhere' with a clear, sweet voice. I watched the fine angle of her face, her clear, lively eyes as she sang. She knew every word of the song by heart. Needless to say she got the part. Smitten, Potty was clapping enthusiastically at the end, completely captivated by her.

'You're perfect as Maria, like a young Natalie Wood. Isn't she perfect, everyone?'

'Yeah!' came the unanimous, enthusiastic response.

When Alex arrived, Potty asked them to try singing

'Tonight' together. Potty listened to the pitch of their voices together, then stopped them.

'No, no, no!' he said. 'Your voices work together but you've got the wrong angle on this song.'

He proceeded to strip the language of the lyrics down to the bone and teach them every nuance and gesture. 'Now try it again.'

I watched them, absorbing their synchronized movements and gestures as they sang: their eyes, their hands, even the way they looked at one another and stood leaning towards each other. I was mesmerized. When they got to the end there was silence. Their eyes met and I was aware of another language going on between them as Tori gave Alex a brilliant, careless smile. Sickened, my mouth went dry with jealousy. I licked my lips, barely able to add to the applause they were receiving.

Tori stood, flicking back her hair, smiling flirtatiously with Alex. All traces of her bad temper had disappeared.

Next, Potty explained the setting of the musical. 'The curtain rises on a bleak scene in a warehouse,' he said. 'Not a word is spoken. In the half-dance, half-mime that takes place there is growing rivalry between two gangs, the Jets, who are American, and the Sharks, who are Puerto Rican. The mood is sinister. The Jets want to clear out the Sharks in a rumble. Now, we'll start with the street scene. Ryan, you're playing the part of Bernardo, the leader of the Sharks.'

Potty started playing the piano softly.

Spider, as Riff, sang, 'Against the Sharks We Need Every Man We Got'.

Alex sang 'Something's Coming'.

The score in his hand shook, his body was taut. His voice rose strong and sure. I forced myself to concentrate on his performance, but I was too distracted. I was wondering what was going on between him and Tori; did he fancy her? I wondered about telling her that we were seeing each other secretly, and to keep her hands off. Instinctively I knew that it would be a mistake. After only this short time I knew enough about her to realise that she might tell Mum and Dad, or worse, make an even stronger play for him.

As soon as Alex had finished Goofer sniggered loudly, and after rehearsals Ryan moved quickly towards him. Alex made for the door, anxious to avoid trouble. But Ryan blocked his way. 'Not in a hurry, are you? I thought we'd have a little chat,' he said mockingly.

Alex looked questioningly at him.

'What I don't understand is why you're at this school,' said Ryan. 'I thought there was a special place for people like you.'

The others laughed.

'Why did you come to this school when there are hundreds of others you could have gone to?' Ryan continued, raising his eyebrows.

Alex's voice rose. 'I was sent here to learn, not to get into fights. Now do you mind letting me pass.'

He walked calmly through them and out of the door.

I stood helplessly, looking after him.

Ryan and the boys laughed.

'You're not funny,' I said to them.

'Sticking up for your boyfriend?' Ryan goaded me.

They laughed again. I left, fuming over what had happened but not wanting any more trouble. Not that I cared what Ryan thought, I wasn't that scared of him – underneath he was a pathetic coward. But Alex was different. I wanted him to know I was on his side – I wanted to talk to him, but I had to go and find Tori. She was getting in the way, and Alex kept slipping out of my grasp.

My efforts with Tori were getting nowhere, and my job was made harder by Sarah. She would appear out of the blue with chocolate, tempting Tori away. I bought Tori treats too, but she preferred Sarah's. Sometimes I thought it would be easier to leave her behind when I went places, but Granny's approval meant a lot to me, and she was putting pressure on me to do the right thing by Tori. No matter where we went or what we did it was obvious that she preferred Sarah's company. I was jealous. Sarah was *my* friend.

I wasn't the only one who was exasperated. Elvie complained about the amount of washing Tori left after her.

'She changes her clothes about five times a day,' she said. 'And she's always hanging around the house gettin'' under your gran's feet and then disappearing just as the dinner's ready!'

'Maybe she has an eating disorder,' I suggested, gossiping.

'Eating disorder me bib! She's a spoilt brat, and the way she gives cheek to your poor grandparents . . . I bet her mother has run away because she doesn't know what to do with her. I know if she was mine I'd give her a good slap.'

'She's just the hired help, isn't she?' said Tori of Elvie, unconcerned when I confronted her later.

'She's not there to be your slave!' I protested. 'Elvie has to work very hard. She works on the check-out in the supermarket all day Saturday. She's a poor widow with a family to support.'

'Why don't you adopt her?' Tori mocked, playing a violin with her finger and thumb.

The development of her friendship with Sarah meant that I was feeling left out, not that I would ever admit it to anyone. Things had changed. Nothing specific that I could put my finger on, just that I wasn't always included in their conversations. Often Tori was invited to Sarah's house and I wasn't. At school they giggled together childishly, exasperatingly, with the boys, often as boisterous as them. I found it disquieting, but when I said this to Sarah she only laughed at me and said, 'You do exaggerate.'

Deep down I knew I was becoming an outsider. So

was Kim, but we didn't have enough in common to form a group of our own.

I finally bumped into Alex, though. He was sitting in the playground. He looked lost in a corner on his own, and jumped slightly when I called his name.

'Sorry, I didn't mean to make you jump,' I said, grinning.

'That's all right,' he said cheerily. 'I didn't expect to see anyone here.'

School had finished for the day. I'd been hanging around in the library. Alex just seemed to be killing time.

His expression was hard to fathom at first, but we chatted. He said he'd been studying hard, and was deep in rehearsals for *West Side Story*.

'No word of your family yet?'

He shook his head. 'No one seems to know anything about their whereabouts.' He shrugged, looking uncomfortable. 'I'd better go,' he said. 'I'll see you soon. We'll talk.' And with a wave of his hand he was gone, leaving me looking after him.

I went and found Tori, who was hanging around by the school gates. 'Ryan says not to leave anything of value lying about when Alex's around, that he nicks stuff,' she said.

I was raging. 'He does not. That's typical of Ryan and his mud-slinging.'

'Why are you so defensive of Alex?'

'Because he's my friend.'

'Yeah, and you'd like him to be more than that, wouldn't you, Beth?' she sneered.

'It's none of your business, Tori, keep out of it!' I hissed.

As we stood looking at one another with open animosity, I made a decision to spend more time with Alex if I could from now on. If only I could get Tori off my back.

12

That evening, after dinner, I went down the sea-front alone. Rounding the corner I approached the Refugee Centre, slowing down with every step, hoping to see Alex. The front door was shut and I didn't want to knock. I considered walking on, but when I turned to cross the road there he was, standing before me.

'Alex!' I stepped back and smiled, desperate to seem calm.

'Beth, hi.' His tone was friendly.

'I was just . . . going . . . I thought that . . .' I stopped, feeling foolish.

'Something up?' His eyes, directly on mine, were gauging me.

'I wanted to see you,' I blurted out.

'Come over here.'

I crossed the road to the park. We sat on the wall. He looked at me, his eyes calculating.

'I was wondering how you got on at the Refugee Agency. Any more news on your family?'

'Not yet. I have to ring them next week,' he said. 'How are things with you?'

'Awful. I have to look after Tori twenty-four hours a day. She's a pain and I can't get away from her. I can't even cycle to school any more because I have to escort her there and back, so I don't get in early. Dad's on his high horse about the homework, won't let me out in the evenings. I pointed out to him that it's not an exam year but he says every year's important.' I rushed on. 'That's why I haven't been able to see you.'

Alex laughed. 'Don't be so worried,' he said. 'I've been busy too. Let's go for a walk to Seapoint?'

My heart thumped irritatingly as we walked.

'How are you settling down here?' I asked him.

'It's better. No one seems to be bothering me at the moment. I wonder if I'm doing a little too well. How long before the trouble starts up again?'

'Maybe it won't,' I said, trying to be reassuring.

'I'd like to believe that,' he said, shrugging.

'Ryan and the others are too busy fawning over Tori,' I said. 'Just enjoy it as long as it lasts.'

'You're right.'

We stopped walking and stood like that, saying nothing, the moon suspended over us, the whole world poised and still. Then suddenly lightning flashed and there was a crackle of thunder. The sky opened and the rain pelted down.

'We'd better go back. Come on,' he said.

I ran with him.

Drenched, we stood motionless in the porch of the Refugee Centre. The rain continue to soak us.

'Let's go inside,' Alex said.

'Won't anyone mind?'

He didn't answer, just led the way up the stairs to a sparsely furnished room at the top of the house. I stood in the middle of the floor, my hair wet and tangled, my clothes stuck to me, not knowing whether to sit on the only chair or remain standing.

Alex shut the door and turned to me. 'Take off your wet things,' he said.

I looked at him, shocked.

'Your jacket and trainers, I mean,' he said.

I removed them. Out of the corner of my eye I saw him watching me.

'Here, sit down.' Gently he led me to the bed.

He sat beside me. I felt awkward as I looked up at him. He moved closer, pushed the hair away from my face with the back of his hand. Our eyes locked.

'I don't think I should be here,' I said hesitantly.

'It's okay,' he said. 'I just want to hold you.'

He put his hand under my chin and looked into my eyes. His hot breath fanned my face as he pulled me against him. On impulse I circled my arms around his neck, and gave him a bear hug to show that everything was okay between us. He kissed me. A thrill shot through me. The world was outside once more and we were here in each other's arms and nothing else mattered. He stretched out on the bed and pulled me down beside him.

I felt it wasn't right to be in his bedroom, on his bed like this. What if someone caught us? 'I really should go,' I whispered.

'There's nobody around.'

His hands were like iron holding me there, his warm body next to mine. He kissed me again, sending an electric current through my body.

A motorbike roared up outside.

'Alex!' A male voice called out, jolting us apart.

Alex pulled away abruptly. He bolted off the bed and went to the window and opened it. I shot up too.

'Yes!' he called out.

'Are you right?' the voice called out.

'Give me a few minutes.'

He slammed the window shut. 'I've got to go – work,' he said.

'I'd better go too. They'll be waiting for me at home.' I was trying to keep the hurt out of my tone as I put my trainers on hurriedly and grabbed my jacket.

I followed him downstairs.

The man on the motorbike was waiting for Alex. He held a helmet out to him.

'See you,' Alex said to me before crossing the road.

I headed for home dejected. Alex hadn't mentioned having a job. And how could he be so formal after the

133

intimacy we'd just shared? What if that was an excuse and he was going off to meet another girl? He could be. My throat tightened, tears squeezed out of my eyes. I walked fast in the rain, feeling stupid.

'Beth!'

I whirled round. Alex had caught up with me.

'Listen, don't worry about anything. I'll see you soon, we'll talk.' He said it as though he meant it.

'Yeah! We will,' I smiled.

He gave me a peck on the cheek and was gone.

I hurried home, confused about my feelings for Alex and even more confused about his feelings for me.

Mum was watching telly. 'What's up with you?' she asked, seeing my blotchy face.

'Nothing,' I said, as casually as I could, before changing the subject. 'By the way, Tori wants to see your studio,' I told her.

'Bring her down tomorrow after school,' she said. She turned back towards the telly and I escaped upstairs for a hot bath and bed. I was exhausted.

The tide was coming in when Tori and I arrived at the studio the following afternoon, the waves racing one another over the rocks, the fishing boats battling against the strong currents. Mum was sitting by her window facing the sea wall, painting. She was so absorbed in her work that she wasn't aware of our presence until I coughed.

She turned and smiled at us. 'I want to capture this scene in all weathers,' she said, her eye on the horizon.

'Come and see,' I said to Tori.

I peered down at her work. The fishing boats were painted and she was adding the fishermen. 'Clever,' I said. 'I can see the wind in the sweep of the tide.'

'Thank you,' Mum said, delighted.

She was thrilled with her new surroundings. I looked around while Tori went outside to admire the men on the building site over the road.

'Has Dad been down to see it yet?' I asked her.

'No. He expresses no interest at all. I've given up discussing it with him.' She smiled, but her disappointment was written all over her face.

Tori came back in. 'I'm bored. Let's go to The Deep End and see if Grandad is there,' she said.

'Good idea,' Mum said, cleaning her brushes and putting them away.

The Deep End was Grandad's local. It was a quiet, spotless pub where he and his friends met for a quiet drink and a game of darts.

I could see him from the door, his head bobbing up and down in a haze of cigarette smoke.

'Hello,' Jim the landlord said jovially from behind his gleaming bar.

Grandad looked up, his eyes wide, his mouth puckering into a smile. 'Hey, how about a drink?'

'Yes please.'

He ordered a Coke each for Tori and me without asking us what we'd like — he'd learnt his lesson — a vodka tonic for Mum, and for himself a pint of Guinness. To our amazement Alex suddenly appeared to clear away glasses.

'I didn't know you were working here,' I said, my heart thumping already.

He smiled. 'Your grandad didn't tell you he got me the job as pot boy?'

'He never said a word.'

'That young Alex is a great lad,' Grandad said. 'He's a grafter and no mistake. I'd no hesitation recommending him to Jim.'

'You didn't tell me.'

'I forgot to, love, sorry.'

I felt sudden extra warmth for Grandad, but I envied the time he spent in Alex's company.

'How's the studio?' Grandad asked Mum.

'Lovely! It's given me a new lease of life,' she said.

'You should set up a little shop there. Sell your paintings when the tourists come in the summer,' Grandad suggested.

'The tourists don't go down that far,' she laughed.

He took a sip of his Guinness. 'Put up a notice, advertize. That would bring you a lot of business. Think of all the punters who'd give good money for a Grace Corrigan original. They'd be dying to part with their money for a souvenir like that. You're one of the best, Grace, a big talent,' he said warmly.

Mum laughed. 'You wouldn't be a little biased, Dad, would you?'

'Maybe, but I'm also right.'

'I think you're getting carried away. Next you'll have me selling handicrafts, traditional Irish songs playing in the background.'

Tori laughed at the idea.

'Come to think of it, Sharon Dempsey does a roaring trade selling fish from her shed down there.'

'I'd need a licence, wouldn't I?' Mum said.

Grandad took a long sip of his drink. 'I'll find out,' he promised.

'I'd also need somewhere to display the paintings. The studio is too small.'

'I'll ask Barney if he'll give you a bit of space in his new hangar when it's finished. It's enormous. You could have a nice gallery at one end, partitioned off.'

'How would I pay for all this?' Mum came back down to earth.

'Get a bank loan on the strength of your commissions.'

Once the idea was hatched it was difficult to shake off. Grandad's face was alight with enthusiasm as he came up with more and more suggestions. Mum listened intently. She was beginning to share his vision; she could turn over a good profit!

'All I need is more investment in material and canvases if I get permission.'

'That's right.'

'I'll have to consult Brian.'

'Why?' Grandad asked.

'Because he's my business partner.'

'Only in the commissions, surely?' Grandad didn't look too happy about that.

I glanced at Tori. She was losing interest, scanning the bar for male attention.

Grandad ordered another round. Tori batted her mascara'd eyelashes, and pouted her lips at Alex whenever he looked our way. She obviously fancied him big time. I caught her eye with a warning look. Much good that would do me. It would probably make her more determined to have Alex for herself. I wanted to push her pretty face in her glass and she knew it.

Tori lingered, maddeningly, for another ten minutes, before slowly draining her glass. 'I'm going,' she said finally. 'It's boring around here.'

'It's time we all went,' Mum said.

'I'll give you a lift,' Grandad offered.

'Beth!' Alex called as I was leaving.

I doubled back.

'Listen, I've seen my social worker.'

'Your social worker?'

'Yes, Tim, he came to take me to meet a newly arrived family from the camp we were staying at in Bosnia, to find out if they had any information about my family.'

'And did they know anything?' I asked hopefully.

'They saw them a few weeks ago, and said that they thought they were going to England.'

'Why England?'

'I don't know.' Alex bit his lip. 'Perhaps it was easier for them to get there.' He smiled happily. 'At least they're alive and well.'

'That's wonderful news.'

'Now all I have to do is find out where they are in England,' he said.

'Good luck! I hope you find them soon.'

'Thanks, Beth.'

'Beth!' Tori whinged from outside.

I went out to find her and Mum.

Tori gave me a sly look. 'You've certainly cheered up,' she said unpleasantly.

I didn't reply, just stuck my head in the air, and we walked in silence all the way home, Mum strolling ahead of us. It was as though there was an electric fence between Tori and me. I couldn't wait for her to be gone from my life.

Tori continued to be as sour as ever around me. Sometimes I could anticipate exactly what she was going to say, even know what she was thinking. Other times she just stared at me like an intimidating stranger. I didn't understand her at all. Her smug silences made me furious.

By the following Wednesday everyone was working hard at rehearsals as a team, the whole of the drama class enjoying the sense of possibility the project had created among us. I found myself seeking out Alex afterwards. It was nothing more than talking, sitting close to one another. He was good company. He was someone I could talk to. Someone who seemed to understand me. We talked for a long time before everyone went home. For the first time in ages I felt excited about life. That night I went to bed early.

I was falling asleep when my mobile rang.

'Hello, Beth.' It was Alex.

'Hi.' I was wide awake.

'I've got a mobile phone. I bought it with my first week's wages.'

'Great,' I said, breathing fast.

I could imagine him in his room, pacing up and down with excitement. 'So how are you?'

'I'm fine. Keeping out of harm's way.'

There was silence. I held my breath.

'Would you like to go to the cinema Sunday night?'

'I'd love to.'

'I'll call for you around seven.'

'Brilliant.'

He rang off. I lay back on my pillows thinking of Alex – impatient to be with him.

The next evening I considered what to say to Mum and Dad. I'd managed to hide my growing interest in Alex from them. I'd have to get their permission to go on a date with him. For once they were together in the living-room, watching the news.

'Alex wants me to go to the cinema with him,' I said casually to them both.

Dad turned down the volume and said, 'Just the two of you or will there be others going?'

'I think it's just the two of us.'

'What time will you be home?' Mum asked.

'I don't know, might go for a pizza afterwards.'

I thought I'd got away with it, but Dad was shaking his head. 'I don't think so, Beth,' he said, turning to me. 'You've got school on Monday, and you're a little young to be out late, alone, with that young man.'

'Honestly, Harry, it's only a film and a pizza,' Mum said. 'We know Alex, we like him. Beth won't come to any harm.'

'It's because he's a refugee, isn't it?' I asked angrily.

His eyes were dark and hooded. 'No, it isn't because of that, but he will have issues. Things to sort out,' was all he would say.

'What has that got to do with him and me?'

He looked at me. His chin lifted. There was deep determination in his voice as he said, 'You're not to go, and that's the end of the matter.'

'I told him I would.'

'You shouldn't have done that,' he said firmly. 'You can ring him and cancel. Now go and tidy the kitchen for your mother.'

'I think you're being a bit hard, love. Beth is very sensible,' Mum said. But I had seen by the set of Dad's jaw that it was hopeless.

He turned back to the television and raised the volume, signalling the end of the matter. In the kitchen I emptied the dishwasher noisily, clattering the dishes together, venting my fury on them. Inside my ribcage my heart had dropped like a stone. I clamped my eyes shut to stop myself from crying. What was I going to say to Alex? I went up to bed, not pausing outside the living-room door to call 'goodnight' as I usually did.

13

Mum threw herself wholeheartedly into her work, going off to her studio each day to paint. She painted the harbour; the majestic white ferry sailing gracefully away against a black, stormy sky, a flock of seagulls trailing it. She painted the pink and blue houses on the sea-front, the redbrick shops of the town behind it, the church spire glittering silver in the late evening sun. She painted the dark boats at low tide, the fishermen in their yellow oilskins mending their nets. In no time at all she had plenty to sell.

'With that kind of output you'll have no trouble paying your way,' Grandad assured her.

'You want to be careful you don't overdo things. You look so tired lately,' Granny said with a worried frown.

One afternoon when I got home early from school Brian Sharkey was just leaving.

'Hello, Beth,' he said awkwardly, as he made a quick exit.

'What was he doing here?' I asked sullenly, when the front door closed behind him.

Mum looked all hot and bothered as she said anxiously, 'Oh, just discussing the studio . . .' She paused. 'You won't tell your dad he was here, will you? He'll only sulk about it.'

'Of course not, but why have him round if you're going to be worried about it?'

'I wasn't expecting him. I could hardly leave him on the doorstep. Besides, I like him, he's interesting, and he makes me laugh. As a matter of fact he makes me feel like a girl again,' Mum said, blushing.

'Mum!' I said irritably. 'I don't want to know.'

Elvie was upstairs when I went to my bedroom. 'Is he gone?' she asked.

'Yes.'

'Thanks be to God. I thought he'd never go. Now I can have me break, I'm gaspin' for a fag.'

'I think he's a creep,' I confided in her.

'Your mum doesn't think so,' Elvie said.

'You don't think she fancies him, do you?' I said, aghast.

Elvie laughed. 'Don't worry. She's flattered with the bit of attention, that's all.'

I wasn't so sure. 'So I've got it all wrong, the way he looks at her and everything?'

'Oh, I've no doubt that he fancies her. But that's a different matter.'

'It's disgusting! He's got a wife of his own and children, for God's sake!'

'When did that ever stop them? I could tell you stories that would make your hair stand on end. Take my next-door neighbours.'

I covered my ears with my hands. 'Don't want to know.'

Elvie got the hint. 'By the way, any news of Tori's mum?' she asked.

'No, after the first couple of phone calls she went quiet.'

'Disgraceful,' she tut-tutted. 'No wonder the kid's weird with such an unreliable mother. What kind of family are they to dump her like that on your poor old grandparents? It's scandalous behaviour. Her father is a right disaster too, by all accounts.'

'She's doing all right at school. Her part in *West Side Story* is bringing her a lot of attention.'

It was true, and Tori, not being one to miss an opportunity, was making the most of her popularity.

'Right enough she has a lovely voice. I've heard her singing around the place.'

'Yes,' I said begrudgingly.

Tori was changing, or something was changing her. I noticed it when I got to Granny's the following Saturday morning and found her tidying her bedroom, Justin Timberlake blaring out of her stereo. Her hunched shoulders and the sullen jaw had disappeared. She had even volunteered to cook a meal for Granny and Grandad, and made a lovely chicken pasta all by herself. She was suddenly all sweetness and light, going out of her way to suck up to them.

Granny was overjoyed that Tori was beginning to take an interest in them at last. Tori spent a lot of time rummaging through the family photograph albums, asking endless questions about the family history that no one had ever bothered to tell her about. I only hoped Granny wasn't getting *too* fond of her.

Tori also began arriving early at school every morning, looking pristine in her school uniform, and she concentrated on her studies.

'What's got into you?' I asked her. 'You seem much happier.'

'I suppose I'm getting used to things.'

'What happened to that boyfriend of yours? You don't mention him much.' I asked sarcastically.

'Who?' She raised a quizzical eyebrow.

'Taylor? Remember?' I joked.

'Taylor . . .' She smiled absently, as though hearing his name for the first time. 'Oh no, that's all over.'

'What happened?' I asked, amazed.

'It just fizzled out, I guess. Long-distance love and all that . . .'

'And you're not upset?'

'Not really,' she said casually.

'But you were crazy about him.'

She shrugged. 'Yeah, well, I'm not any more,' she said,

unconcerned, painstakingly painting her nails. 'I won't be seeing him when I go back home.'

I left her in her room and went to talk to Granny. But after twenty minutes we heard the front door slam. Tori had skipped off mysteriously.

'She's probably gone to the library,' Granny said. 'She says she spends a lot of time there.'

So it was all over between Tori and Taylor. But what about Alex? Would she go after him seriously now? I tried to put that thought out of my head, but it wouldn't go away. I was terrified.

Alex was working most evenings at The Deep End, charming the regulars with his efficiency and good manners. He seemed to be settling down too. Since I'd had to turn him down on the cinema date I hadn't seen as much of him as I'd hoped, but I'd thought about him a lot. I had been stupid in asking Dad's permission. I seemed to be doing the wrong thing all the time. Well, I wouldn't make the same mistake again. Next time I would just go.

Encouraged by Grandad, Mum decided to hold an exhibition in the Parochial Hall. We were all busy helping her prepare for it. I wrote the invitations, and Mum sent them out. On the night the hall was filled to capacity with friends and important business acquaintances, mostly of Brian Sharkey's. Mum, in a fabulous black satin suit, charmed buyers with her work. Tori and I served the drinks. Mr Tutty, our bank manager, was most excited about the paintings. He commissioned one of Dun Laoghaire harbour for his office. A friend of Brian's wanted one of Galway Bay.

Tori was enjoying herself, developing a taste for champagne, knocking it back like water when she thought no one was looking. Her eyes were glazed. She was getting drunk.

'Haven't you had enough?' I said, disapprovingly.

'Get lost, Beth,' Tori said rudely.

'I don't think you should have any more,' I advised.

'Why not?' she said rudely.

'Champagne makes you drunk really quickly and gives you an awful hangover.'

'That's my problem,' she said rudely.

'Any champagne left?' Becky asked.

'Not much,' I said, throwing Tori a filthy look.

Becky got the message and took over, giving Tori a lecture.

I moved off, grateful that the place was full of people so she wouldn't be able to get back at me.

Dad made a brief appearance at the end of the evening. He barely acknowledged Brian.

Mum confronted him about it on the way home. 'There was no need to be rude to him,' she argued.

'He's not my friend,' Dad said in self-defence. 'It's you that has the soft spot for him!'

'I have not,' Mum denied, flushing slightly.

From then on the atmosphere in the house grew more tense. Dad was increasingly unhappy about the length of time Mum spent away from home. She avoided his questions by not talking to him. Though he knew more about what was happening in Dun Laoghaire than anyone else, he seemed uncertain about what was going on in his own home. I knew it was only a matter of time before there was a big explosion between them. I wanted to be as far away as possible when that occurred.

Mum was going to Galway for a weekend to study the light over Galway Bay, and take photographs. On the day she got all dolled up, putting on her lipstick, tracing the outline of her mouth with it, a frown on her forehead.

'I think it's time I had a face-lift,' she said.

'What!' I said. 'You look great, Mum, really glamorous.'

'I don't feel it, I'm getting old.'

'No you're not,' I laughed. 'You're the youngest, prettiest Mum of all my friends' mums.

She stared at her reflection in disbelief, pulling her face this way and that, yet pleased with my compliment. Then she left, instructing me to be sure to look after Dad while she was gone. I promised I would, but I couldn't stand the thought of staying in the house by myself. The place was would be like a mausoleum without Mum.

After dinner I started my homework, but abandoned maths in favour of taking poor lonely Trudy for a walk. The night was cold. I walked quickly, Trudy trotting along beside me. The tide was coming in, washing over the rocks. Slivers of light from the yacht club lit the waves. I threw stones for Trudy to chase. She tore along the strand, disturbing the gulls from their sleep. They flew up, shrieking in protest. Once past the point I doubled back, calling her to heel. Near the Refugee Centre I loitered, my eyes on the road, while she nosed around. Cars went by. I thought about knocking on the door and casually saying I was passing . . . Would Alex invite me to his room again? Would I go? If I did, would we do it? I knew he would get more insistent and wondered what I was going to do about it. Why was I so scared of that? Plenty of girls I knew were having sex. It was no big deal according to them.

I was about to turn back when I saw Alex come running towards the centre. Tall and lithe, his skin glistening in the lamplight. My heart skipped a beat, but he hadn't seen me. Just as I was about to cross the road Tori came teetering out of the door of the centre in stilettos. Alarm bells rang inside me.

'Hi,' she called, peering up at him in the dim porch light, a crooked smile on her face. 'I've been waiting for you,' she said, giving him a playful shove.

'Oh!' he said, surprised.

I watched them hunched together in the semi-darkness before they went inside.

I stood on the empty pavement, my mind suspended in disbelief. What did she think she was doing? Was she drunk? Alex hadn't invited her, had he?

Devastated, I dragged myself home and finished my homework, hardly able to keep my mind on it. I didn't have to wait long before Dad came home. Becky turned up later. I heard the sound of her music, and her laughter vibrating through the wall as she talked on the phone to one of her friends. I wanted to tell her what I'd just seen, anxious for her to soothe my crushed .feelings, but something stopped me. Alex was my secret. I looked around my bedroom and felt the four walls closing in on me, trapping me. I wanted to cry but no tears came. I feel so isolated I wrote in my diary, '*Why is everything going wrong for me? I'll kill Tori when I get my hands on her.*'

But I didn't let on to Tori that I'd seen her. I was afraid that she might tell me that she and Alex were an item.

Mum's return was a welcome relief. I hugged her as she came through the door.

'It's good to have you back,' I said, and took her bags upstairs.

As I came back down I heard Elvie say to her in a low teasing voice, 'Mr Sharkey phoned and left a message for you to ring him.'

I didn't hear Mum's reply. In the kitchen she produced her sketches. She'd done some really energetic work and she was tired. When Dad got home later that night I heard them arguing in their bedroom. I could hear the rising anger in Dad's tone, though not the exact words, and the sound of doors slamming.

Next morning he was still in a rage. Mum was getting ready to go out.

'Good morning,' I said, pretending that nothing was wrong.

Neither of them made any effort to reply. Mum was first out of the door for once.

As soon as she closed it after her Dad said, 'I bet she's gone off to see *him* again.'

'Who?' I asked, pretending I didn't know what he was talking about.

He ignored me. 'I've watched them together. He never takes his eyes off her. She talks to him more than she talks to me.'

'But *you* don't talk to *her*,' I said. 'And you're hardly ever here,' I called after him as he got ready to leave for work.

'Less of your cheek, young lady,' he said, and slammed the front door behind him.

Things were very wrong between them. They no longer seemed to be able to communicate without having a row.

'He resents the fact that I've got a life of my own,' Mum said tearfully to Elvie later on.

'I know what you mean,' Elvie sympathized. 'My fella used to hate me going out to work, too. He'd rather have me cleaning up after him, or in the nest, if you know what I mean.'

Mum frowned, indicating me.

I left the room depressed with the two of them. I was tired of Mum being unhappy, and Elvie was too old to be discussing sex publicly, never mind doing it.

Mum tried to make it up with Dad by cooking him elaborate meals, but often he would return home from surgery too late to want them. Things were going from bad to worse. I told Becky how worried I was about the two of them.

'Why?' she asked, surprised.

'They might split up.'

'Don't be daft, of course they won't.'

'Suppose Brian lures her off somewhere?'

'You've been reading too many romances. Mum's just lashing out at Dad for neglecting her. It's as simple as that.'

I wasn't convinced. 'But it's awful what's happening to them, we have to do something.'

'Keep your head down, don't interfere,' she advised. 'I don't like it any more than you do, but quite honestly I'm sick of the pair them.'

I faced her. 'You wouldn't care if they separated.' I said, turning away from her.

She grabbed my arm and swung me round. 'Things aren't always what they seem.'

'Meaning?'

'We don't always know what's going on between people.'

'I know that they hate one another.'

153

She calmed down. 'No they don't. They're going through a bad patch, that's all. It happens in all families. They'll sort themselves out.

14

In the school canteen Tori threw her sandwiches in the bin. 'I'm putting on weight,' she moaned, taking a yoghurt from her bag.

Sarah threw her eyes heavenwards. 'You're as thin as a reed,' she declared.

I sipped my Coke, casting glances at the door every time it opened, hoping Alex would walk in.

'Expecting somebody?' Sarah looked at me suspiciously.

'No!' I lied.

Ryan and Goofer came in, and headed straight for our table as if they knew we'd be there.

'So, things are going well for you?' Ryan said to Tori, his eyes straying all over her.

Tori sat up, alert. Sarah glared at her but Tori took no notice. Suddenly she was full of chat, expressing her opinion all over the place, laughing gaily at the stupid jokes Ryan made.

'Are you going to the disco Saturday night?' he asked her.

'Depends,' she said, batting her eyelashes at him meaningfully.

'On what?' he asked.

'On whether her granny will let her out or not!' Goofer sniggered loudly.

Tori glared at him. 'My gran lets me do more or less what I like.'

'So, are you glad you came here now?' Ryan asked her.

'Yes, it's nice to be part of a family again, and to have new friends.'

He took a swig from his Coke bottle, and moved closer to her. She stuck her chest out, and flashed her eyes at him.

On the way out I said to her, 'What on earth were you flirting with that eegit for? He's nothing but low-life.'

She looked at me long and hard. 'And you'd be a connoisseur of low-life, wouldn't you?'

'Meaning?' I asked coldly.

She scoffed. 'Oh, squeaky-clean Beth, never steps out of line! But look who you're chasing . . .'

'What d' you mean?'

'Don't come the innocent with me. You're off down the sea-front every evening after Alex. You wouldn't give Ryan a second glance but you're after that gypsy.'

'Who are you to call anyone a gypsy? You're chasing him, too. I saw you with him the other night.' I hissed at her.

'We were practising our parts in *West Side Story*,' she hissed back.

'Yeah! Right!' I brushed past her and marched off.

In English class, as Mr Higgins launched into a discussion about constructing sentences, I sat seething at Tori's cheek. How did she really feel about Alex? She must fancy him!

The rehearsals gained momentum. Tori couldn't keep her eyes off Alex, or her hands, either, when she got the chance. Everyone noticed it.

Sarah said to me on the way home, 'Tori's very flirty around Alex.'

'She's like that with all the boys,' I said flippantly. But I was furious.

'I'm sure she's after him,' Sarah persisted, giving me a sideways look.

I bit my lip to stop myself agreeing with her. I didn't trust Tori where boys were concerned, especially now that she and Taylor were finished, that particular nugget of information I decided not to pass on to Sarah.

On Saturday evening, when I went to Granny's to practise the piano as usual, I found her anxious. She hadn't seen Tori all day. When I said I hadn't seen her either, she got panicky. She took her responsibility for Tori very seriously. Seeing the worried look on her face, I did my best to reassure her.

'I'll find her, don't worry, and I'll get her to come

home,' I promised, leaving to look for her, livid with Tori for upsetting Granny.

I headed for the snooker hall where Ryan and his gang hung out. Known among the locals as the Hellhole, it was a dark, dingy shed near the West Pier. I went into the gloomy hall with trepidation. Ryan, Spider and Goofer were there, and so was Tori, standing with Ryan, watching Goofer and Spider compete. She had a bottle of beer in one hand and a cigarette in the other.

Seeing her getting along so well with these thugs made me furious. Ryan spotted me.

'What're you doing here?' he asked.

Tori jumped back.

'Granny's looking for you. She's worried about you,' I told her.

I could tell Tori had had a few beers. She said defiantly, 'I'm hanging out with my friends.' Her eyes were wide and belligerent.

'You'd better go home, you shouldn't have gone off without telling them where you were going.'

Tori's eyes narrowed. 'Oh, come off it, what's the big deal? I'm used to going off on my own at home.'

'This isn't Toronto. You're a guest here, and you're Granny and Grandad's responsibility.'

'We're just having a laugh, not doing any harm to anyone,' Tori said.

'Yeah, we're just having a laugh,' Ryan repeated, basking in the attention. 'No law against that, is there?'

'Yeah!' Tori agreed, swaying.

I looked at her. She was acting even more daring under Ryan's protection. What was with this bad-girl attitude? Was she trying to shock me? In a way I *was* shocked: she seemed out of control. Ryan was obviously delighted with the animosity between us.

'Come on home,' I asked her.

They both laughed as if they were sharing some hilarious joke in which I had no part. Ryan said, 'Chill out, and have a drink.' He held out a can of beer.

'No thanks. And I think you've had enough, too, Tori,' I told her.

Ryan put his arm around her.

'And you can back off,' I said to him.

He laughed slyly and went to join the others at the pool table.

I pulled Tori to one side. 'You're not with him, are you?'

'What if I am?' She raised a defiant eyebrow.

'He's bad news. He'll get you into trouble.'

'Oh, you're always going on about him. You're obsessed with hating him and you expect the rest of us to feel the same.' She brushed her hand across her forehead in frustration.

'You don't know him like I do,' I said.

'Hey! Listen to this!' she burst out. 'Beth doesn't approve of the company I'm keeping, she's trying to drag me away.'

'She's jealous 'cause she's never invited here,' Goofer laughed.

I walked away, calling over my shoulder to Tori, 'Suit yourself, but you'll have nothing but trouble with them, and I'm telling Granny and Grandad where you are.' I got out my mobile.

She followed me, grabbed it from me. 'You're a jealous cow, Beth Corrigan. You can't bear to see me enjoying myself, can you?' she shouted.

She stumbled out of the pub after me. I reached out to prevent her from falling. 'Get off me!' she yelled, shaking me off.

'Tori!' Ryan came after her.

He held his hand out to her. She went back to him and took it.

'You'd better take her home if you don't want trouble,' I said. 'And give me back my mobile.'

'Get lost.' She staggered off with him.

'Yeah, you heard her,' Ryan shouted belligerently after me.

That minute I hated Tori as much as I hated Ryan and his mates. I walked home downcast, lonely, wishing I would bump into Alex. He'd definitely cooled off since he'd begun rehearsals with Tori. That was another reason to hate her. She hadn't just turned Granny and Grandad's lives upside down, she'd messed up mine as well. There was nothing I could do about it except have it out with Alex.

I decided to wait until after rehearsals the following

Wednesday. We were rehearing in earnest now, and though I was little more than a member of the Jets I was eager and keen, putting my all into my part. Alex was so absorbed in his role that not even the jibes from Ryan's gang seemed to faze him.

'Alex! Wait!' I called out as he hurried off.

He stopped. I caught up with him. He looked tired and preoccupied.

'Are you working tonight?'

'No, it's my night off.'

I surprised myself by saying, 'Want to go for a coffee?'

'Okay, but I have to study first. See you at eight?'

'Fine.'

He went off and I ignored the gibes from Sarah and Kim. Tori was nowhere to be seen.

Later, Alex and I sat in the dim lamplight of The Rainbow Café, alone at last, the silence awkward. I knew I had to say something about seeing him with Tori, but I suppose I was scared of his answer. Afraid I'd break down and cry all over him and make a fool of myself if the response was what I expected it to be. I could hardly pick up my cup, I was so panicky.

'I saw you with Tori at the centre the other night,' I blurted out.

It was only a few seconds before he answered, yet it felt like a lifetime.

'We were rehearsing.' He looked at me. 'What did you think? That I was with her?'

Eyes down, I reached for the coffee cup to delay my answer.

'Is that what all this is about? Beth, look at me.'

'Yes.' I felt silly saying it aloud.

I raised my eyes.

His eyes were wide with incredulity. 'I don't believe it,' he laughed, in mock horror.

'It's not funny.' I could feel my face flame with embarrassment.

I couldn't tell him that seeing him and Tori together had affected me so badly.

He bit his lip and glanced quickly down at his cup, then burst out laughing again, shaking his head at the absurdity of it.

'Well, what was I supposed to think?'

'That's what you get for spying on me.'

'I was not spying on you,' I said hotly.

He was still shaking his head, the whole incident a big joke to him.

'I'm going home.' I scrambled out of my chair and made for the door. He followed me.

'Beth, come back.'

'What's so funny about thinking that you might be with Tori? She's obviously attracted to you!'

'It was the expression on your face that I was laughing at.'

I shrugged, but I relaxed a little.

We walked along without saying anything. My arms

dangled awkwardly by my sides, my feet felt like lead. I had made a fool of myself and now felt cut off, set adrift by the awful silence, and the terrible emptiness inside me. If only Alex was the talkative, extrovert type.

'Goodnight,' I said huffily when we got to my house.

Alex turned to me and, without warning, took me in his arms. I stood transfixed. We stayed like that for what seemed a long time. When I went to say something his kiss drowned out the words. He kissed me again, a long, greedy kiss, and ran his fingertips down my throat, lingering on the base of my collarbone. I held my breath. Not daring to move for fear of breaking the spell. When we did eventually draw apart he was smiling.

'Does that answer you question?' His eyes on me were gentle.

'Yes, it does.'

'Do you feel better now?' he said in a husky voice.

I nodded, too overwhelmed to say anything else. We walked to my house in silence, our arms around one another.

'When can we see each other properly?' Alex asked, his eyes anxious. 'I mean, go on a date?'

'Soon, I'll phone you.'

The hall light came on.

'Make sure you do,' he said, kissing me again.

I skipped up the steps, my heart fluttering like a feather.

15

I got home from school the following Tuesday to find
Mum packing her bags. I could tell that she'd been crying.
Her eyes were red rimmed and she flushed a little when
I came into her bedroom.

'I'm going to stay with Linda for a while. Until things
calm down here,' she said wearily.

Linda was her friend from her college days. She lived
in Cork. Mum hadn't seen her for a long time.

'Did you have another row with Dad?'

'Yes.' She looked at me. 'We need to give each other
some space. It'll give us both a chance to cool down. I'll
take my paints. Perhaps I'll find something stimulating to
paint while I'm there.'

I didn't cry until she'd left, I'd promised myself
I wouldn't. As soon as her car disappeared out of
sight I sat on my bed and stared at the four walls,
then turned my face into my pillows and wept.
Becky must have heard me because moments later
she came into my room, sat down and put her arms
around me.

'They're being a bit thoughtless around us at the moment,' she said crossly.

'Maybe they can't help it,' I said.

'Maybe not, but they're behaving like children. They really piss me off sometimes.'

'What if they really do hate one another?' I looked down at my clenched hands.

'Of course they don't. They'll be fine,' she said. 'Everything will be all right. Get some sleep, you'll feel better in the morning.'

I didn't feel tired so I sat at my computer playing games for something to occupy my mind before going to bed. Then I lay in the dark, unable to sleep. At some point I heard Dad's car turn into the drive, then the scrape of his key in the lock and his footsteps on the stairs.

Later, I heard a muffled choking sound that repeated itself coming from Mum and Dad's bedroom. I got up and stood outside their door with my hand on the doorknob, unsure whether to knock or go back to my room. Softly I opened it. Dad was lying across their bed still in his suit, his head buried into his pillow, crying. I closed the door and crept back to my room, feeling terrible.

Everything around me seemed fraught with danger, full of secrets, even the sky itself seemed to be falling in on me. Finally I slept and dreamt that the walls were crumbling around me, the roof was caving in, every structure collapsing, all that was so familiar vanishing, including myself.

Next morning Dad was in the kitchen drinking a cup of coffee, staring out at the garden.

'Hi Dad,' I said, giving him an uncustomary kiss on the cheek.

'Good morning,' he said.

The silence stretched out between us.

'Are you all right?' I asked, anxious about him.

'Fine,' he said.

'Would you like something to eat?' I asked.

'No thanks, I'm not hungry. You make sure to have some breakfast before you go to school, though.'

'I'm not hungry either.' I looked at him. 'I miss Mum.'

He put his hand on my shoulder. 'I know, love, but we'll manage without her for a couple of weeks, you'll see.'

That evening he shuffled around miserably. There didn't seem to be anything to say. I stayed with him until he went into the living-room to watch the news, then I took a yoghurt and went up to my room.

'You can't stay in your room all the time,' Becky said later on. She was in the kitchen, doing some washing.

I looked at her. 'Dad's miserable. We'll have to tell Mum.'

'No.' She was emphatic. 'They have to sort it out between themselves. We can't interfere. The best thing you can do for them is to act normal, get on with it.'

'Act normal when Mum's not even here! How can I? What if she's gone for good? What'll we do then?'

She gave me a withering look. 'God! You're so dramatic! Of course she isn't gone for good. Look, stuff happens, it's not the end of the world.'

'It is for me.'

Becky laughed. 'Pull yourself together, Beth,' she said unsympathetically.

I was angry with her. How could she be so indifferent to a crisis like this? She was right about one thing, though. Nothing we could do would make it better. We'd have to let them solve their own problems. Next day I phoned Mum to find out how she was. She sounded fine, said she was enjoying herself, that Linda had taken her sightseeing and was spoiling her.

I could tell that she was putting on a brave face. I didn't tell her I missed her. Instead I kept my voice upbeat; told her we were all managing. I didn't say anything to my friends either. I was too ashamed. But I could hardly keep the truth from Tori. When she asked where Mum was, I decided to tell her.

'Are you sure she's not gone off with that Brian?' she asked, her eyes lighting up at the idea of it.

Outraged, I said, 'How can you say such a thing? Mum wouldn't do a thing like that.'

'I'm not so sure. She's an attractive lady,' she said. 'Brian obviously thinks so.'

'She's with her friend Linda,' I snapped at her. 'I've been on the phone to her there.'

The idea of Brian being Mum's lover was too awful to contemplate. In fact, Brian as a lover defied even my vivid imagination. He gave me the creeps.

'You've been reading too many romantic novels,' I said, furious with Tori for sowing a seed of doubt which was already beginning to niggle; I remembered that I'd phoned Mum's mobile. She could have been anywhere.

I dreaded going home from school. I hated the stillness that awaited me when I opened the front door. The house was empty and deserted without Mum. Each evening I stood in the kitchen and wondered what it would be like if she were to leave altogether. At night I would huddle down into my bed, like a shipwreck on an island.

Elvie was there when I got home after rehearsals on the Wednesday.

'I made you a bit of dinner, lasagne, your favourite.'

'Thanks, Elvie, but I'm not really hungry,' I said automatically. Food was the last thing on my mind.

'You have to eat something. You don't want to be moping around with an empty stomach.' She was dividing the food on to the plates.

It did look appetizing. I realized I was starving after all.

'How are you getting on, anyway?' Elvie asked when we sat down.

'I wish Mum was back home.'

'Stop frettin', Beth. Your ma'll be back before you know it,' she said, chewing carefully.

'Maybe something terrible has happened between her and Dad, and she hates him. Tori thinks that she might have gone off with Brian Sharkey.'

I looked across at Elvie, frightened now that I'd voiced my worst fears.

She laughed. 'Trust that silly eegit. 'Course she hasn't. Your mum wouldn't do anything stupid like that.'

I wasn't reassured.

Elvie changed the subject. 'How's that refugee boy gettin' on?'

'OK.' I told her all about his part in *West Side Story*.

'Lovely! I must go and see it. You like him, don't you?'

'Yes, I do, but so do all the girls,' I confided to her. 'Including Tori.'

'She's no competition. She couldn't hold a candle to you in looks and personality.'

'You're biased,' I said, laughing.

'That's true.' She laughed too.

Still, she'd cheered me up.

On the Friday Dad was kept busy with patients and meetings with other doctors. Granny insisted I went to her house for dinner.

'So how are you?' she said, leaning one hip against the counter.

'It's lonely without Mum.' Without warning my eyes filled with tears and I stared at the ground trying not to cry.

She put her arms around me. 'She'll be back soon. Nothing's going to keep her away from you for long, I promise you.'

Dad came to collect me. He had dark circles under his eyes, deep lines around his mouth. Granny and he held a private conversation in the living-room while Tori and I did our homework in the kitchen.

It didn't take Sarah long to find out that Tori was seeing Ryan. She caught them snogging behind the bicycle shed. She was furious with me for not telling her about it.

'You knew it was going on.' She tossed her hair back theatrically. 'Why didn't you say something. I thought you were my friend.'

'I am,' I protested.

'You could have stopped her.'

'I tried,' I said feebly.

'Duh! You could have warned me. Now I've lost him,' she wailed, her chest heaving. 'Why did she have to pick him?'

'I've no idea,' I said truthfully.

'I thought she was my friend, too. Why did she have to steal him? She could have anyone she wanted. She's a slut.' Sarah turned red, but looked defiantly at me. 'I don't care if she is your cousin.'

We were sitting in the café near my house, drinking cappuccinos. Sarah was puffy-faced from crying. Through the window behind her I suddenly caught a glimpse of Tori on the other side of the road. I tried to distract Sarah, but for some reason she turned to see what had caught my attention and saw her too. Before I could stop her, Sarah had leapt from her seat and was out of the café. I followed her, trying to limit the damage. But even I was amazed at her venom when she attacked Tori, who was typically nonchalant.

'You weren't really ever with Ryan Godfrey, not properly,' Tori reminded her.

That was the worst thing she could have said. In one sentence, Tori shattered Sarah's dream world and made her recognize the real situation for what it was. After another screaming fit at Tori Sarah began to cry, huge gulping sobs. I tried to comfort her by saying that Tori and he weren't boyfriend and girlfriend, only friends. She wouldn't listen and choked out, 'I'll never forgive you for not telling me, Beth.'

She refused to talk to me, slamming down the phone when I tried to talk sense into her. As far as she was concerned I'd betrayed her friendship and her trust.

'We're not friends any more, Beth,' she declared dramatically.

'*I'm an outcast,*' I wrote in my diary. '*And it's a very lonely feeling.*'

171

That was an understatement. I hated Tori for all the heartache she'd caused. Did she care? Not one little bit. She knew about my rows with Sarah and was enjoying the fact that she was the centre of attention as usual. She was spending more and more time with Ryan. They were together as often as possible, either at the cinema, or in the snooker hall; though she never told Granny or Grandad that she was with him. She knew they'd stop her.

Her few weeks of playing the good girl had come to an end. She'd become a shopaholic, too. It was designer labels or nothing. She had enough money from the undisclosed sums regularly sent by her mother to support her addiction.

It was as if Tori had discovered that there was an interesting world out there and she intended to conquer it. She'd taken up drinking in a big way, coming into school in the mornings with her head exploding. The slightest noise, a slammed desk-top, or a raised voice, and we had to scrape her off the ceiling. I was desperate, not knowing what to do: torn between telling Granny and Grandad what was going on and not causing them extra worry.

'You're drinking too much,' I challenged Tori at school one day.

She gave me a contemptuous look from under her lashes. 'No I'm not. I only have a drink to make me forget all the horrible things in my life.'

'What things?'

'Oh everything. Mum hasn't been in touch. She's forgotten all about me,' she added with a grimace.

I didn't know what to say to her. She suddenly seemed small and pathetic. For a moment I felt sorry for her, but I couldn't take on her problems. I had enough of my own. Sarah was speaking to me again, just about, but she was still furious with Tori over Ryan.

This newly discovered world of Tori's included other, older boys, too, some of whom she was beginning to really take notice of. Soon she would drop Ryan for someone more sophisticated. She already had her eye on Scott.

'He's more mature, and he has prospects,' she said, with a wicked gleam in her eyes.

In the middle of all my despair, Mum came home. She walked into the kitchen in a new sheepskin coat, startling me as I sat at the table, studying.

'Mum!' Tipping back my chair, I rushed to hug her. 'It's so good to have you back, we really missed you!'

She looked different – a bit plumper and kind of glowing. Beautiful.

'Oh darling,' she said, stroking my hair. 'It's great to be home. I missed my girls. How's everything been?'

I wasn't about to tell her about the latest dramas – not yet at any rate.

'Fine, Mum, we're all fine,' I assured her.

She took off her coat and went slowly into the kitchen to sit down. She suddenly looked exhausted.

'I'll go and phone Dad to let him know you're home, he'll be thrilled,' I said to change the subject.

'He knows, I spoke to him on the phone,' she said. 'I'd kill for a cup of tea, love,' she added, and I rushed to put the kettle on.

'Tell me what you did at Linda's,' I asked, curious about everything that had happened while she was away.

She told me about Linda's family, the friends and places she'd visited with her, about the sketches she'd made, the photographs she'd taken.

I told her about my progress in school.

'How's *West Side Story* coming along?' she asked.

'Great. Tori's really good,' I said, leaving out the row I'd had with her and Sarah over Ryan.

Dad came home early. He had an enormous bunch of flowers for Mum. He fussed over her, making her sit down, getting a cushion for her back. Maybe things were going to change for the better now.

16

Tori came to stay with us while Granny and Grandad went to Marbella for their annual holiday. She continued to go off on her own whenever she got the chance. No one except me realized that she was drinking too much until she came in late one night reeking of alcohol and falling around the place.

Dad was still up. 'You're drunk,' he said, a look of amazement on his face.

'No I'm not,' she said indignantly.

'What do you think you're playing at?'

'Nothing,' Tori said with a sour expression.

'You're a disgrace, I want to know the name of the pub, I want to report the licensee,' he persisted.

Tori had a fit of the giggles.

'Stop it at once, young lady,' he said, catching her by her shoulders. Then he let her go so suddenly that she almost fell. I'd never seen him so angry in all my life.

Tori backed away, scared. 'Leave me alone, I don't have to listen to this.'

'Yes you do. There's no excuse for this kind of

behaviour. I won't tolerate it. Now get to your room!'

'I hate you all. You make me sick. I'm not staying here,' she shouted.

'You have no choice.'

'I'm going to find Mum, stay with her.'

'You're a silly girl if you think that drinking is cool,' Dad said, more gently. 'You'll end up in trouble if you don't stop. Now get to bed and get some sleep.'

In the bedroom she said to me, 'You needn't stand there judging me, you can get lost.'

'Don't you blame me if your bad behaviour gets you into trouble,' I snapped at her. But she was off on one.

'I'm sick of the accusations, the way you all try to make me feel bad. It's Tori did this, Tori did that, Tori don't do this, don't do that.'

'It's for your own good.'

'Well, you can't control me! I want to be left alone to do my own thing, lead my own life.'

'You mean you want to be left alone to drink.'

'I don't want your dad shouting at me.'

'What do you expect?'

'Oh, get lost! Leave me alone.'

The next evening I met Alex coming out of the parish hall.

'What are you doing down here?' I asked.

'Helping to install the lighting for the disco on Saturday night. Barney asked me to. Will you be coming?'

'Yes, we're all going. It should be good fun. I'm looking forward to it.'

'Great! I'll see you then.' He smiled.

On Saturday, returning from piano practice, I caught sight of Ryan. He was watching me from the doorway of the snooker hall. As our eyes met he turned away. I caught a flash of Tori's jacket as she stepped back into the dimness. Later, when I tried to reach her on her mobile to see where she was, it was switched off. She hadn't come home by the time I was leaving for the disco.

Sarah and Kim called for me. Sarah was wearing a new low-cut pink top and black cut-offs. Kim wore a black top and black mini-skirt and platform shoes. They looked very sophisticated.

When we got to the hall Scott was in the office acting as cashier.

'Hi,' I said, surprised to see him. 'Are you running the show?'

'Just giving a hand with the supervising,' he said, smiling as he took our money. 'By the way, I got a place at UCD,' he added.

'That's great news. Congratulations!' I said, really pleased for him.

The hall was packed. Some people were already drunk; a few of the boys were prancing around showing off their six-packs, their faces contorted by the strobe light. The whole place thumped with the beat of the music, the heat enveloped us. Girls as sleek as cats in tight jeans and strappy sandals swayed sexily to the beat, others romped around. Ryan, Goofer and Spider were huddled in a dark corner. I tried to ignore them as I passed by. 'Want some?' Ryan held out the joint he was smoking.

'No thanks. Where's Tori?'

They exchanged glances, but no one spoke. Ryan took a long toke, his eyes on me dark and unfocused. I shook my head and went to find Sarah and Kim, who had started dancing. I joined them.

As we all danced Alex appeared out of nowhere. The music throbbed. I moved stiffly, aware of Ryan's tense, wary, unblinking eyes roaming the hall. Alex was a brilliant dancer, his narrow waist rippling to the music, his hips swaying.

When the music stopped I looked around for Tori. There was still no sign of her. But as Destiny's Child floated out of the speakers. I began to relax, made myself forget Ryan's wary eyes. We were dancers in the mob, checking our moves on the floor, no one taking any notice of us. When the number finished I turned and spotted Tori before she saw me. She was leaning against the wall, a ring glinting from her naked midriff, her micro denim skirt showing off her long legs, her mouth curving as she tipped a bottle to her lips. She was as tough looking as the boys, and just as drunk.

I went over to her. 'Tori, are you okay?' I asked, concerned.

She looked at me with her mocking green eyes, taking some kind of pleasure in my anxiety, then threw her head back and took another slug of beer. As her hair fell back I noticed a bruise over her right eye.

'Did someone hit you?' I asked, suddenly worried for her.

She grunted, and her eyes slid sideways as she hunched forward defensively.

'Did Ryan hit you?' I persisted.

She took another swig of her drink. 'Wouldn't you like to know?' She said, slurring her words.

Ryan walked over. He stared at me, moody and bitter. 'Keep out of this,' he growled at me. 'It's none of your business.' I took a step back.

Unconcerned, Tori lit a cigarette. Her eyes narrowed defiantly above the flame as she looked at him.

He grabbed the match, flickered it in her face then flung it away. 'You're coming with me,' he barked at her.

Her head snapped up. 'Get away from me,' she cried, stepping out of his reach.

He grabbed Tori. Her hands shot out. She hit him across the face; her nails snagged his skin.

'Bitch!' He howled, taking a step back then grabbing her again.

'Leave her alone,' I shouted at him.

Fury rose up in him. 'Get lost, Beth Corrigan.'

'You heard what she said,' Alex's voice suddenly shouted

above the din. Taking Tori by the hand he steered her protectively away from Ryan.

Tori preened, fluttering her eyelashes, tossing her hair back, shaking her hips to the music. Alex had no choice but to dance with her. Ryan glowered at them. We were all up dancing, hurtling round the hall. I was pretending to enjoy myself with Sarah and Kim. Goofer and Spider were dancing like idiots, while Alex looked uncomfortable with Tori. Across the dance-floor I spotted Scott, arms folded, watching us. And Ryan, on the other side, stared at Tori. Fuming, he jerked back his head and, teeth bared, shouted, 'Useless fucking gypsy,' at Alex.

Right on cue, and like a raging monster, Goofer came forward, his fists closed, eyes alight with excitement. Alex's face hardened. There was a dull thud of blows and both reeled back, falling. I stood still, not daring to move my down-cast eyes, too terrified to look up, my heart pounding wildly like a drum.

A lifetime passed. Goofer was up first. He took another lunge at Alex as soon as he got to his feet. Alex stumbled and fell.

A circled formed around them.

'Stop!' I screamed.

But in that split second an explosion ripped the air. Everyone leapt back with fright. Flashing blue lights appeared at the back of the stage. Sparks showered down around us as a series of sharp bursts went off. Five shot up from behind the band. Loud bangs exploded in deafening waves.

Everyone was panicking, making for the door. I covered my head with my arms, and pushed forward. The chill night air outside hit me as I escaped the smoke and suffocating smell of sulphur. There was no sign of Tori in the crowd that had gathered. I looked around wildly, my teeth chattering as fear gripped me.

'Where's Tori?' I shouted to Sarah.

'She must be still in there,' Sarah called out to me.

I ran back inside, squinting through the smoke for a glimpse of her. 'Tori!' I screamed.

'Here!' Her cry was like the screech of a gull.

I found her crouched against the wall, hunched up in fear. Blood pumped inside my head as I moved rapidly, feeling the heat of the flames. Cramped, terrified, I held my breath, trying not to inhale the fumes as I reached for her.

'Take my hand, follow me, don't look back,' I said, grabbing her.

Flames leapt around the stage. I was starting to feel giddy. She was lagging behind. 'Come on!' I dragged her forward.

A noise exploded against me. Transfixed, I felt a white heat searing into the leg of my jeans. I screamed, twisted away from it before it burnt my skin. I covered my head with my arms. The sparks singed them. Everything was crashing around us.

Near the door there was another loud explosion followed by a crash, then darkness. A blast of heat hit me. Acrid smoke burnt my eyes, clouding my vision. I couldn't find the door. Alex was coming towards me, squinting at me through the smoke. His eyes were feverish in the light of the flames.

'Don't look at the fire,' he commanded.

'Tori!' I cried out in horror, but my tongue was too thick for my voice to come out loudly.

Alex moved like a wild animal – faster than I've ever seen anyone move in my life. Staggering, he hauled Tori out, commanding her to 'Walk!'

She was losing consciousness, zigzagging crazily with her head lolling. Using his body to shield us he moved forward. I focused on the door, the smoke making me choke. My legs were weak and my head swung giddily. Blood pounded in my ears.

A sudden gush of air rushed up to meet me. I was outside at last. My eyes felt heavy. I was going to faint.

Alex's hands gripped my shoulders. His face was streaked with sweat and black with smoke. 'You're okay?'

I rubbed the back of my scorched leg. My jeans were torn; there were burns on my flesh.

Glass was everywhere, empty bottles and puddles of beer. Ryan was standing before us, his eyes fierce in his blackened face.

'You did this,' he said to Alex.

'What!' Alex said, amazed.

'You did the wiring. It's your entire fault.' He turned to me. 'Forget him, he's a loser,' he said. His eyes were bloodshot, his mouth twisted sideways in an ugly slit. He looked at Goofer. There was a plan being put into action between them.

Like a wolf, Goofer bared his horrible teeth – they looked longer and more ferocious than ever. 'Yeah! You're to blame.'

Scott appeared. 'Get out of here and don't be so bloody stupid,' he said to them both.

Turning away, they disappeared into the darkness.

'Take no notice of them,' he said to Alex. 'You okay?' he asked me, putting his arm around me.

'Yeah. You?' He was pale and there was a rasp in his voice.

A clanging sound marked the arrival of the fire brigade.

'Step back!' Scott's commanding voice jolted everyone.

I looked up into the face of a fireman as he stepped forward to marshal us all to one side. An ambulance arrived, then another. Tori was taken into the first – she was as floppy as a rag doll and needed immediate medical attention. A paramedic helped me into the same ambulance, his voice seeming very far away. I could hear what he was saying as I tried to hold my head up, but it kept lolling on my neck.

Dad was among the doctors waiting for us in Outpatients.

'You're going to be all right,' he said, his arm around me, propping me up.

He was coolly professional as he examined Tori first, then me. I knew he was having difficulty keeping calm.

'Superficial,' he said, checking my arms and legs, moving them gingerly.

'Oh Dad!' I started to cry, the tears stinging the cut on my face.

His hand reached out and touched my check. 'Don't cry, sweetheart. You've had a lucky escape.' He cradled me against him for a second, then moved on to examine the others.

'Tori?'

'We're keeping her in for observation. Smoke inhalation.'

'Ohmygod!'

'She's fine.'

'Can I see her?' I asked.

Dad shook his head. 'Tomorrow.'

A nurse appeared to treat my injuries. Twenty minutes later I went to find Dad.

'Mum's on the way to take you home. It's going to be a long night here for me,' he said.

Mum and Becky arrived. Mum rushed towards me. 'Thank God you're safe.' She folded me in her arms.

They helped me out to the car, and Mum gave Scott a lift home too. There was no sign of Alex, or any of the gang. They were being treated in separate cubicles of Outpatients.

At home I lay in bed, my head buzzing, keeping me awake. Gazing into the darkness, listening to the familiar sounds, I could see the flames of the fire. When I fell asleep I dreamt of the fire: Ryan, laughing like a hyena, his menacing eyes watching me unblinking; Goofer leering at me, his mouth curved like a crocodile's, his teeth open to devour me; Spider, crawling all over me. In my dream Tori looked like a frightened little rabbit as the huge yellow flames reached out to envelop her. I woke up screaming. Mum was by my bed, her hand holding mine, a glow of anxiety in her eyes as she reassured me over and over again that I was all right, and that no one had been seriously injured.

Dad drove me to the hospital to see Tori next day. She had a wad of bandage over one side of her face and she was as pale as a ghost. She was lying very still.

'Tori!'

She looked at me blearily.

'How are you feeling?'

'Rotten. Like I have the worst hangover ever,' she groaned.

'Dad says you'll be home tomorrow,' I said, trying to cheer her up.

'I don't have a home.'

'You're staying with us, remember?'

'Great! she said sarcastically. She started crying, big tears slipping down her cheeks.

'Don't cry,' I said, moving closer. 'Does it hurt?'

'No, they gave me something for the pain. Stop fussing. 'Is Alex okay?' she whispered.

My eyes narrowed. 'Yes . . .'

'Was he looking for me?' she asked anxiously.

'Not as far as I know.'

Her eyes swivelled away, as if it was my fault, then she turned her face to the wall.

My throat was tight. I swallowed hard to get rid of the lump in it.

'I've screwed up big time.' Her face contorted. Tori looked so frail lying there.

'No you haven't.'

'You don't have to lie to me to make me feel better.'

I stood watching her breathing as she fell asleep. She was alive, that was all that mattered. Dad drove me home. I waited for a lecture but it never came.

Scott called over to see how we were. He seemed to have recovered completely.

'I'm fine, but Tori is still in hospital,' I told him.

'She had a lucky escape,' he said.

'You all did,' said Mum.

'Want to come to over to my place to watch a video?' he asked me.

'Go on,' Mum said, 'it'll take your mind off things.'

I shook my head. I felt too wound up to enjoy a video,

and in spite of her being such a pain, I was also too anxious about Tori.

Tori came home the next day, looking forlorn, her normally sparkly eyes dead. The spirit seemed to have gone out of her and I suddenly felt guilty that we hadn't bonded, and that I hadn't been more understanding of her. I vowed to make more of an effort.

17

The following week at school we were all gathered in the Assembly Hall, except for Tori who wasn't well enough to return. Mr Higgins stood before us, Sergeant Byrne by his side.

'I'll get straight to the point,' Mr Higgins said. 'I'm sure you realize that you're all very lucky to be here, after the fire, and lucky that no one was seriously hurt. It could have been a very different story.' His palpable anger made him a powerful presence.

'Yes, Mr Higgins,' we said in a subdued tone.

'The damage to the hall is considerable. No one seems to know anything about it, much less take responsibility for it. You all seem to have had sudden lapses of memory.' His eyes on us hinted at our guilt. 'One thing we do know is that alcohol and drugs were being consumed in large quantities.'

There was total silence.

'I expect you all to co-operate with the Gardai in their enquiries, and to be truthful to them.'

'Yes, Sir,' we chorused.

Sergeant Byrne stood up. 'We shall be questioning everyone who attended the disco on Saturday night. It's entirely up to all of you how long it will take. Arson is suspected.'

We all filed out, terrified.

'Do you think the cops have someone in mind?' Kim asked.

'Don't know,' I said. I had a terrible churning in my stomach.

'How's Tori?' Sarah asked, noticing my worried expression.

'She's home and on the mend.'

'Will she be all right?' Kim asked.

'Yes, she needs to rest that's all.'

Sarah smiled in relief. 'She's a dark horse that one, but I wouldn't wish her ill . . .'

I linked arms with her. 'I'm glad you've stopped fighting,' I said. 'It's one good thing to come out of this mess at least . . .'

The house was as quiet as the grave when I got home that evening. Tori was asleep, Mum said, and warned me not to disturb her. Hoping I wouldn't bump into Ryan, I took Trudy down to the sea-front, on the off-chance Alex would be there, but there was no sign of him.

When I got home there was a police car parked outside the house. A group was sitting round the kitchen table:

Dad and Mum, and Sergeant Byrne, Dad's friend, at the head. Dad had a look of strain on his face.

'Ah, there you are, Beth,' he said, smiling encouragingly. 'Sergeant Byrne would like a word with you.'

'Hello, Beth, how are you?' Sergeant Byrne said cheerfully.

'Fine, thanks.' I looked from one to the other.

'That's good. I suppose you know why I'm here.' He took a notebook from his pocket.

I nodded and sat down.

'I believe you attended the disco last Saturday night?'

'Yes.'

'I'm sure you were very scared,' Sergeant Byrne said.

I admitted that I had been.

'Beth, I want to talk to you about what happened before the fire broke out.'

Mum sat biting her lip, a concerned expression on her face. She kept glancing at Dad, who was looking down frowning.

Sergeant Byrne said, 'You witnessed the row between Alexandru Dragoje and Ryan Godfrey.'

'Yes.'

Sergeant Byrne checked his notes. 'Alex hit him, is that right?'

I whipped around. 'Alex was acting in self-defence. Ryan wanted a fight. It was him who started it. He was drunk, acting stupid, being rough with Tori. Alex told

190

him to leave her alone. Ryan started picking on him, pushing him.'

'I hear Alexandru is having a bad time at school in general, being picked on and that.'

'Ryan Godfrey hates him, so do his pals Goofer Keegan and Spider Conroy. Alex is different. He's popular with the girls because he's good-looking and he's polite to them. Ryan doesn't like that. It makes him and his mates feel threatened. Because he's from a different culture, they don't understand him.' I lowered my voice as I said it.

Sergeant Byrne gave me a curious look. 'So you'd say that you have got to know Alexandru pretty well?'

I could feel myself blush, wondering what Sergeant Byrne was driving at. 'Well enough,' I said, wishing I knew him better.

Mum came to my rescue. 'Alex has being doing a bit of work for me down at the West Pier.'

Sergeant Byrne nodded, then turned back to me. 'Do you think Alex is the kind of boy who would bear a grudge, perhaps?'

'Alex would never start a fire, if that's what you mean,' I said, indignantly.

Sergeant Byrne didn't let up. 'Goofer Keegan said that he was the one who got you out safely.'

'That's a lie. Can't you see through them? It was Alex who brought me and Tori out.' I was almost weeping with frustration as I shouted into his face, trying to make him understand.

'Why would Goofer want to lie about it?' Sergeant Byrne scrutinised me.

There was a brief silence. I was frightened. I wanted to leave the room but I wanted to set the record straight.

'Alex's just a kid,' Dad said. 'Probably scared out of his wits. He's on his own, too, should have someone looking after him. You're not going to charge him with anything, are you?'

Sergeant Byrne shook his head. 'We'll talk to him, see what he has to say. We need to hear his side of events.'

Nobody spoke. They all looked at me, the expression in their eyes doubtful. I lost my temper. 'I wish Alex had split Ryan's head open, really given him something to complain about.'

Mum turned to me, shocked. 'Beth! That's a terrible thing to say. You don't mean that, you're upset.' She turned to Sergeant Byrne. 'She's still in shock.'

I stood up to leave.

Dad glared at me. 'Beth, this is no way to carry on.' He said to Sergeant Byrne apologetically, 'Kids don't always understand what they're saying.'

I wrenched free. Sergeant Byrne stood like a wall in front of me: tall and grey like a threatening bird of prey. 'We'll get to the bottom of it,' he said. 'Find out how the fire started. You needn't be afraid,' he added. 'It might have been faulty wiring. We have to check out everything.'

Mum's eyes were damp, as if she were about to cry.

'They're only children, they don't understand,' Dad said as I squeezed my eyes, trying not to cry.

'No, unfortunately they don't,' said Sergeant Byrne.

Dad saw him out. When he came back into the kitchen he gave me a stern look.

'Now, Beth, I think you should go to your room and rest.'

I escaped gladly. I had plenty to think about. Ryan had seen his chance to get rid of Alex by blaming him for starting the fire. Everything that had happened was beginning to seem unreal.

My legs ached. I threw myself on my bed. I had to go and warn Alex.

That night I waited until everyone was in bed then stood in the corridor, listening. All was quiet. I sneaked to the back door.

'Beth!'

I spun round. Mum was standing behind me, pulling her dressing-gown around her. 'Where are you going?' There was sharpness in her tone, an impatience that was new.

'Out!' I said defiantly.

'Out where?'

'Sarah's. I have a necklace she needs to borrow for tomorrow,' I lied.

Mum hesitated. 'Don't be long,' she said. 'And come

straight home.' She regarded me suspiciously for a minute before going back upstairs.

Trembling with anxiety, I put Trudy's lead on. 'Come on girl,' I coaxed her – she was half-asleep, and didn't want to be disturbed.

I closed the door behind me, and almost ran down the road pulling Trudy along after me. I stopped, waited. I set off down the sea-front, my jacket wrapped tightly around me, my face hidden in its hood. The sea was a line of silver under a sliver of moon, the rocks and crevices of the pier big, dark shapes against it.

As I approached the Refugee Centre I could see a light on in the front room. I knocked and waited in the porch. A woman in oriental robes answered the door, her wrists jangling with bracelets.

'Is Alex in?'

She looked me up and down. 'Wait here,' she said and padded off to get him.

The sitting-room door was open. A few people were sitting around a fire watching television. Alex came downstairs, his wrist bandaged.

'Beth!' He said it as if he'd been waiting for me, but he looked tired and drawn. 'Sprain,' he explained, lifting his arm slightly. 'It's not too bad.' He plucked nervously at the bandage.

'Sergeant Byrne came round.'

'I know,' he said softly. 'He was here too.'

'It's Ryan and the gang spreading lies.'

'Don't worry, he didn't charge me with anything,' he said, the muscles of his face stiffening as he forced himself to keep calm.

'Will you have to go away?'

'Why should I?' His eyes flickered, his jaw jutted out.

'They're out to get you.'

'I'm not scared of them.'

'They're rough, Alex. You don't know what they might do next.'

He held my gaze. 'I'm not going anywhere, Beth.' He dug his nails into the palms of his hands. 'I have to stay – there's school, the musical, and my job in The Deep End. I need that job, and I like it. Why should I have to go? I've been moved around enough. I'd rather stay around and face them.' There was a grim determination on his face.

Seeing my worried look, he said, 'You think I can't look after myself, don't you?'

'I know you can. It's just that Ryan and Goofer are trouble. They've got in it for you, Alex.'

He looked as though he were about to explode. 'They are losers! I can't let them intimidate me, Beth. I've made up my mind, I'm staying here. I want to give it my best shot no matter what happens.' His words tumbled out, distorted with emotion and tears he was holding back. 'You do understand that I have to stay?'

'Yes.'

He put his hands on my shoulders. 'It'll be all right, Beth.'

I closed my eyes, smelling the sea on him, and pine forests far away in another land, determined to be there for him. We were in this together.

When I opened my eyes again Alex was looking at me, trying to give me one of his careless, happy grins. 'Stop worrying about me,' he said light-heartedly.

On my way home I met Elvie coming out of the bingo hall. She was done up to the nines, her hair magenta pink and shining, her lips perfectly outlined in her favourite purple lipstick.

'What's wrong, Beth? Are you all right?'

I told her all about the fire and that Alex was being blamed for it. She had already heard.

She walked me home. 'Look, I know this has nothing to do with me,' she said. 'But if I were you I'd keep away from Alex, for now anyway.'

'I thought you liked him.'

'Oh, he's lovely, but there's trouble around him. Let things cool down, and don't aggravate the situation by hanging around him. Go home to your family, sweetheart, you look as if you could do with a good night's sleep.'

She meant it kindly, I know. But I couldn't forget about Alex, no matter how hard I tried. How could I desert him now? I truly believed that if I could help him things would work out all right.

The next morning Mum talked to Tori about Sergeant Byrne's interview.

'They're trying to blame Alex for starting the fire,' Mum said. 'Just because he helped with the electrics.'

'He's just an easy target,' Dad said. 'The truth will come out sooner or later.'

18

Dad insisted that Tori stay with us until she was completely better. She and I were still off school so we went to The Rainbow for a coffee to get out of the house, and relieve the boredom. Ryan and Goofer arrived just as we were about to leave.

'I was doing my nut worrying about you,' Ryan said, sitting down beside Tori.

Tori kept her distance, her arms folded across her chest. She was looking at him as if seeing him for the first time.

'You didn't even phone to see how I was.'

'I was going to.'

'Yeah, right!'

'You needn't believe me if you don't want to.'

'I don't,' she said, her voice cracking and her face white underneath her make-up. 'Come on, let's go,' she told me.

Ryan tried to pull her back as she went to get to her feet.

'Get off me.' She pushed him away.

'Leave her alone,' I said.

He looked at me. 'This is your doing. You put her off me,' he snarled.

'No she didn't!' Tori raised her voice. 'You deserted me when the fire broke out. You ran off.'

'I searched everywhere for you,' Ryan protested.

'That's right!' Goofer said. 'The stage end was burning, we couldn't get back in.'

Ryan said, 'That end of the hall is destroyed.' He turned to me. 'Faulty electrics they think. Alex is in trouble, he wired it up.'

We ignored them and left.

'Tori, wait! Can't we talk, work something out? You know I'm crazy about you,' Ryan said, coming after her in desperation.

Tori shook her head. 'Sorry,' she said, 'I have a life to live that doesn't include you.'

'Slag!' he spat, clenching his fist.

Her hand shot out. She hit him hard, right across the face.

'Ouch!' he roared, his face contorting.

Sarah and Kim appeared. Ryan went back inside the café, cursing.

'What's up with Ryan?' Sarah asked, dying to find out what had been going on.

Tori buried her face in her hands. I thought she was crying but she was laughing, shaking all over. 'I don't know how I ever fancied him, he's so awful,' she said.

199

On the way home Tori said to me, 'I've been such a pain, I'm sure you're all sick of me.'

I put my arms through hers as a friendly gesture. The truth was I was sort of warming to her.

'If Mum really wanted me she'd have come back for me by now.' Tori added, sadly. She looked like a lost child.

'She's still on tour. Probably hasn't got any definite plans yet, she'll let you know as soon as she does,' I consoled her.

'Don't make excuses for her, Beth. She can't be bothered with me. I know, it's all happened before.'

I could see the strain in her eyes as she tried not to cry. My heart went out to her. I squeezed my arm against hers. 'I want you to stay here.'

'You're only saying that because you feel sorry for me,' she said.

'No, I mean it.'

'Seriously?' she looked hopefully at me.

'Yeah! Seriously.'

That night I watched her sleeping in the spare bed in my room. Her hair was spread out over the pillow and her face was flushed. With her eyes closed and her arm flung out she looked innocent, like a child. I told Mum and Dad what she'd said about Colleen.

'She's not a bad kid underneath the tough shell she shows to the world,' said Dad.

'She should be with her mother by rights, though,' said Mum.

'Did it ever occur to you that it might have been good for her to be with us in a family environment rather than the mess she calls home?' Dad said, frowning. 'You know, I'm surprised that Vicky didn't do more to help her.'

'I'm going to phone her. The poor kid's had a raw deal and I'm going to let Vicky know,' Mum said.

'She won't like your interfering,' Dad muttered. 'And it won't make a blind bit of difference.'

We all noticed a change in Tori over the next couple of weeks. She stopped drinking and buried herself in her studies, and *West Side Story*. She practised her singing all the time, stopped hanging around the snooker hall, and refused to take Ryan's calls. Though she returned to Granny and Grandad's, she spent more of her spare time with me. She was enjoying her studies. Mr Higgins told Dad he was pleased with her progress. Dad was delighted. To celebrate he treated us all to dinner at Marco Polo's, our favourite Italian restaurant in town.

I was on my way home from walking Trudy the next evening, my head down against the ice-cold wind, when a car swished to the curb and stopped beside me. It was Scott. He rolled down the window.

'Beth, how's it going?'

'Fine!' I said, leaning against the car. 'How's college?'

He grimaced. 'Lectures all day. I spent most of the first week getting lost looking for the different lecture halls.'

'You like it though?'

'Yeah, but I've a stack of work to do.' He indicated a ton of books crammed into a canvas bag on the passenger seat.

'I missed you round the place,' I said, suddenly realizing that it was true.

Scott gave me a look. 'Want to come over to our house for a while? I have the place to myself. Mum and Dad have gone on a pilgrimage in thanksgiving for my results.'

'I bet they're really proud of you.'

'I suppose so,' Scott said modestly. 'They don't say a lot, you know what they're like . . .' He paused. 'Well, will you come?'

'Why don't I bring Tori with me?'

'Brilliant,' he said, but without enthusiasm, and backed up into his driveway.

But Tori wasn't very keen to go to Scott's and so I ended up cancelling it. She and I spent the evening watching DVDs and drinking Tipperary spring water.

One evening when I got home from school Mum was sorting through her clothes, pulling out sweaters and jeans, trying on this and that.

'I've put on weight. None of my clothes fit me any more.'

I looked her up and down. She was plumper all right, but at the same time she was tired-looking and a little pale.

'You have put on a bit of weight,' I said. 'Mum, are you okay?'

She smiled at me. 'Beth, I have something to tell you,' she said.

'You've sold one of your paintings for a fortune.'

She shook her head. 'I'm going to have a baby.'

'What!' Startled, I looked at her. 'You can't be.' I could hear the shock in my own voice.

'Well, I am. It wasn't planned – not at my age . . . but I'm pleased. I hope you are too.'

I was dumbstruck. I couldn't get my head around this astonishing news.

'Aren't you going to say anything?' she asked.

'I'm in shock.'

'Me too. I must say a baby was the last thing on my mind. I thought this extra weight was middle-age spread,' she laughed, pointing to her stomach. She blushed as she regarded me. 'I know you need time to take it in, but I hope you'll be happy about it. It would mean a lot to me.'

'Oh, Mum, I am happy for you.' I went to her and put my arms around her. 'You'll be all right, though, won't you? I mean, you won't be ill or anything?'

'Of course not,' she reassured me. 'I'll have to be careful, but there's nothing to worry about. Dad's making sure of that. It was a shock to him, too. The last thing he wanted was a new baby to look after, but he's getting used to the idea.' She smiled confidently. 'He's being very sweet, actually.'

'It's great that you two are getting on again.' I smiled happily. 'When's it due?'

'March, I think. I'm about four months pregnant – and to think I didn't even know!'

Excited, I told Tori the next day at school.

'Is it Brian's?' she asked immediately, her eyes shining with intrigue.

Gobsmacked, I looked at her. 'Of course it isn't, how could you say such a thing?' I said indignantly.

She backed off seeing my expression, but she got my imagination whirling again. All during French I sat thinking about the possibility of Brian Sharkey being the father of Mum's baby. I wondered what Dad had thought. He wouldn't be treating her so well if he suspected the baby wasn't his, would he? I pushed the horrible idea out of my head. It couldn't be true.

As it was, the constant rows had ceased and it was peaceful in our home again. Dad was gentle with Mum in a new sort of way. He insisted she must rest a lot. He didn't want her to paint much, though. She got bored doing nothing. Each evening, as soon as he got home from work, he would go into the living-room to check on her. Often, looking at her, his face would be seamed with worry lines, though he always sounded cheerful. He made us understand that she was not the same woman who'd given birth to us, she'd been much younger then. Now it was harder for her, and more risky. I noticed that they were being careful with one another, as if there was a great mystery between them.

Becky was the only one upset by the news of Mum's

pregnancy, though she managed to hide it from her and Dad.

'She's too old!' she said harshly to me. 'It's not right.'

'I think it's great. Dad's being wonderful to Mum and I'm happy. Things could have been so different.'

'Dad's really pleased about the baby, isn't he?' I said later to Mum.

'Yes, I think he is.' She smiled. 'It's going to be tough, but it will be a new start for us. It's his child too, after all.'

His child! I sighed with relief. 'That's brilliant, Mum!' I said, hugging her.

Mum must have noticed my worried expression, though. 'What is it, Beth? Is there something on your mind?'

'No . . . I mean . . . it's just I thought may be Brian Sharkey . . .' I trailed off.

Mum's eyes widened. 'What?' She was aghast. 'You thought I was carrying Brian's baby, did you?'

'No! I mean, yes. I didn't know what to think.' I couldn't tell her that Tori had put the idea in my head.

'Oh, Beth,' she said, coming to me, taking me in her arms. 'You poor love.'

'I'm sorry, Mum,' I said glumly.

'No, I'm sorry, I'm the one to blame,' she insisted, 'to have put you through all that unnecessary worry. That really makes me sad.' She looked away in miserable silence. 'Now don't worry and don't take too much notice of your Dad's fussing, he's over-anxious.'

I let Mum have some peace and solitude and went to fill in my diary. I wrote in it. *'I think a new baby in our house would be wonderful.'*

Life changed dramatically for Mum. She painted occasionally at home but she didn't get down to her studio at all. Dad wouldn't let her. However disappointed she was she didn't voice it. She focused on looking after herself and the baby. I did my best to help her, and Elvie was coming round more often for support.

'There's Granny and Grandad, too,' I reminded her.

'They have enough on their plate with Tori.'

'She's really cleaned up her act, lately, though,' I reminded her.

'I know, love, but they're not getting any younger, they need some time to themselves.'

I hadn't thought of that.

Elvie came in each day to clean and keep things in order. Once a week she gave the house a 'good going over', as she called it. Every Friday evening she did our grocery shopping, and arrived with her car laden with bags. I helped her put the groceries away. Sometimes I went with her to shop. She knew all the staff and we had a good laugh.

'Ruth's coming to do your mum's hair. I thought a new hairstyle might cheer her up,' she told me on the way home one Friday evening.

Ruth was Elvie's eighteen-year-old daughter and recently qualified as a hairdresser.

'She's got a scooter now, you know. Me heart's in my mouth every time I see her takin' off on it, but it means she can do nixers in the evenings, and make a bit of extra cash for her holidays.'

'That's a great idea,' I agreed.

'I'm worried about her,' she confided. 'She's seeing this rap singer. Out all hours. Came in at three o'clock this mornin'. I said to her, what time do you call this, and she only said "bed time" and sidled off. She can be a cheeky young wan.'

'She's grown up now, isn't she Elvie?' I said. 'It's just a matter of getting used to it.'

'You sound like a oul' wan yourself, but I suppose you're right.' Elvie gave me a wry look.

The following morning I heard the sound of a scooter bouncing into the drive. A pretty girl with bright blonde hair arrived with a large vanity case, and a helmet. It was Ruth.

'Howya!' she smiled. 'Where's the victim?'

She showed Mum elaborate styles in a hairdressing magazine she had.

'Just a trim and blow-dry?' Mum said.

Ruth, sighing, took out some lethal-looking scissors from her accoutrements. In spite of her non-stop chatter she was a clever stylist, and Mum looked beautiful with her new, jagged cut.

* * *

Mum's pregnancy had a strange effect on Tori. She was almost reverential in Mum's presence, and was always offering to do something to help her. Tori hadn't touched any alcohol for weeks. I think the fire at the disco had frightened her more than she let on. She spent quite a bit of time in our house; the rest of it was spent in Granny and Grandad's, keeping out of trouble. I stayed in as much as I could, too, to be on hand if Mum needed me for anything.

Scott had been in touch a few times. He phoned to ask me to go bowling.

'I can't leave, Mum,' I said guiltily.

Mum heard me. 'You should go. It's no fun being stuck here with me.'

But it wasn't Scott I wanted. It was Alex I was yearning for. I wanted to go out on a proper date again with him, but there was always something stopping us. I had homework, and helping in the house. He had his part-time work, and he was keeping a low profile. The main problem was that Dad seemed to be doing everything and anything to keep me away from him.

19

Mum had asked me to keep an eye on her studio, so I went there regularly to check on it. And that's when I had an idea of how Alex and I could meet – without Dad knowing. At school I got a message to Alex, asking him to meet me at the studio after dinner one evening.

I was on my way there, walking along the path by the sea wall, when I heard footsteps behind. I turned to see Ryan – who had appeared from nowhere, seemingly. He caught up with me.

'Well if it isn't Miss Goody Two-Shoes!' he called, grinning. 'This is a surprise. You shouldn't be on your own,' he tut-tutted in mock reproach, delighted at my discomfort. 'Are you waiting for someone?'

I knew to be careful not to mention Alex. 'No,' I said, walking on past the studio.

'Cool, aren't we?' he mocked, the sound of his laughter carrying out over the water. 'Ah, Beth . . . can't we be friends again?'

'We never were.'

He stopped in his tracks. His grin stretched from ear to ear as he said creepily, 'I used to fancy you, you know?'

I shivered, wishing he'd go away. But he was coming stiflingly close. I tried to step past him, but his bulk blocked my path. I flinched. We eyed each other like enemies. My impulse was to shout at him to let me pass. I decided against it. There was no one within earshot and it would make him angry.

'So your boyfriend's not coming out tonight?'

'I don't have a boyfriend.'

'I've seen you with that gypsy. They're a curse, you know, those damned Romanian gypsies. They'll take over everything in the town if they're let.'

'Is that what your da told you?' I asked.

'I've seen it with my own eyes.'

'I keep telling you he's not a gypsy.'

'Well whatever he is, he's different.'

'No he isn't. He is one of us now and he has every right to be here.'

Ryan gave me a look of contempt. 'You don't care what happens to our town, do you?'

I was shaking as I stared at him, hardly daring to breathe. My revulsion must have shown in my face because he said, 'Don't look at me like that.'

'Like what? You can't stand anyone who isn't like you.'

I could see the anger in his eyes, but there was

something else, something predatory too. I thought better of antagonising him any further, so I said, 'Excuse me, I've got to go.'

He reached out grabbed my arm, holding it in a vice-grip. 'What's the rush?' he said.

My heart was thumping. I glanced up and down the pier. There was no one in sight.

'What's the matter with you? I'm trying to be friendly.' The sharpness in his voice startled me. 'You're not frightened, are you?' He opened his eyes in mock surprise; there was a mean glare in them.

I was terrified, and he knew it. I tried to edge away but he wouldn't let go of my arm. He carried on looking at me, then he stepped closer. 'You could come to my place. The folks are away.' His heavy breath was on my face; his eyes on me were furtive.

'No thanks.' I made to walk off.

He moved with the speed of a springing cat, blocking my way, catching me by my shoulders.

He smiled. 'We could have a drink, just chat if you like.' His glassy eyes were trained on me. 'There's booze and I've got some dope.'

A shiver ran up my spine. I turned my head away but he lunged forward to kiss me.

'Get away from me.' My voice was strangled.

'Or you'll what? What'll you do?'

'I'll scream,' I said shrilly.

He laughed. 'No one will hear you,' he said calmly.

'I have to get home. They'll be wondering where I've got to.'

'No they won't.'

My heart was hammering. There was tightness in my chest and my head was pounding, but part of me didn't really believe that he would harm me. He was pretending, playing a game, trying to frighten me. Don't panic, I told myself. If I stayed calm I could persuade him to let me go.

He was closer than ever. 'There's nothing you can do,' he said, looking at me from beneath his lashes. 'I've got the advantage.'

Really scared now, I backed into the wall, praying that someone would come along and rescue me.

'Get lost, Ryan!' I shouted.

'Shut up,' he hissed, lunging at me, rage in his eyes. My hands scrabbled, trying to get at his face to scratch it.

He gripped me as hard as he could. 'You want it as much as I do,' he growled.

'No!' I was crying.

'Shut up,' he hissed, his hand over my mouth. 'You've got to be quiet.'

I looked up at his revolting face, the square teeth, and the sneer on his upper lip. Suddenly, he was grappling with the zip in his jeans. I whimpered knowing what he was going to do, and that I was powerless to stop him.

'Save your breath,' he sneered.

I stood transfixed, too scared to move, smelling

the rank sweat off him. There was a sudden, screeching cry.

'What was that?' He stood tense and alert.

A huge bird flew overhead, its wings whirring frighteningly like a warning. He crumpled and loosened his grip on me as he looked up with a nervous toss of his head, as suspicious as a criminal on the run. In that split second I bolted, my heart pounding, my feet flying.

'Bitch!' he hissed after me.

I kept running. I could hear him pounding after me. I slipped down to the level crossing, and hid behind the yacht club wall. I heard him run past, and waited until the sound of his footsteps died away, then I ran up the path towards the car park, panting, with a burning pain in my chest.

'Got you.' He sprang out from nowhere.

I stumbled and fell. 'Ouch!' I was crying.

'Stop whining.' He was breathing heavily, his face murderous. From out of the dark Alex stepped in front of him.

'What are you doing with her?' he growled.

Ryan jumped back, confounded. 'You're not the only one she fancies,' he sneered.

Alex clenched his fists. 'Get away from her,' he warned.

As they faced one another I tried to clear my brain and think of something to stop them, but nothing came.

There was a great tearing noise as Alex attacked Ryan, ripping open his shirt.

'Gypsy!' Ryan called in a burst of exultation.

'Don't call me that again,' Alex threatened through gritted teeth.

Ryan had wild look in his eyes. 'Or you'll do what?'

Alex lunged forward, wild with anger. He swung at Ryan, who stumbled backwards. Straightening himself, Ryan came after Alex, his teeth bared, sweat drops on his forehead and upper lip. Alex caught him, hit him again.

'Ouch!' Ryan staggered, his eyes full of feigned astonishment, blood spurting from his mouth.

'Touch her again and I'll break every bone in your body,' Alex said, his fist balled ready to hit him again.

'You've got it wrong, gypsy, she was begging for it,' Ryan shouted, wiping the blood from his mouth.

Alex swung him round like a rag doll, and put him down. He was about to use his fist but Ryan ran. Alex chased after him, caught him by the legs, and rammed them up against his chest. Ryan screamed, flailed about. Alex just bent his knees harder. He pushed him to the edge of the steps. Ryan looked up at him, his eyes rolling with fright.

'Don't, don't,' he screamed, his voice reverberating round the rocks.

Alex leaned over him.

'Stop!' Ryan screamed again, his voice echoing hollow.

Alex let go. In that instant Ryan scrambled to his feet. He stabbed his fist in the air. 'I'll get you for this.' He hobbled off.

Alex's clothes were torn. He had long scrapes down his cheeks.

'He asked for it,' he said, when he got his breath back.

Shaking and shocked, I helped him up, and took him over to Mum's studio. I made a pot of tea and cleaned his cut with damp tissues, assuring him that Ryan would live to tell the tale, knowing very well that more trouble lay ahead.

20

I removed my wet shoes and left them inside the door, crept upstairs to the bathroom and locked the door, ran a bath, squirted in lots of bubble bath and soaked in it, then scrubbed myself clean until my skin hurt.

'Beth!' It was Mum's voice.

'Yes.'

'Come on out, you've been in there long enough.'

I got out, dried myself, examined the purple bruises on my arms inflicted by Ryan, and put on my night-dress. Mum was waiting for me. She noticed the bruises on my face.

'What happened?' she asked anxiously.

'Nothing, I fell on the way home, that's all,' I said lamely.

'Are you all right?'

I assured her that I was and got off to my room before she could ask any more questions. In bed I heard the sound of a police car siren. For a second I thought it had stopped outside our house. Terrified, I waited for a knock on the door. It didn't come. I got out of bed and crept to the window, pulling the curtain aside to look down into the eerily silent street. Nothing! I switched off the light and went to sleep.

In my dreams Ryan's face emerged pale as the moon. I could see clearly the way his eyes shifted, and his insistent hands tugging at my clothes. I woke up terrified, replaying the scene endlessly in my head. Finally, I gave up trying to sleep. I switched the light back on and got out my diary. Endless questions spun around in my head. What if it got out that Ryan had tried to rape me? Dad would go mad and things would get worse all round for everyone, including Alex. Nothing felt safe, not even my bed. Why did my life seem so scary all of a sudden?

I wrote how I felt in my diary, but didn't dare write down the actual events that had taken place. Next morning I woke up with a thumping headache and my shoulders ached. Dad was shaving in the bathroom. He turned as I opened the cabinet for a painkiller.

'You're very pale. Worried about anything?'

I shook my head and fobbed him off with the maths test that I'd clean forgotten about as an excuse.

I didn't see Alex at school. In the maths class I sat brooding over my test, exhausted, wondering how long I could keep going, wishing I could sleep for a month to block out the whole episode of the previous night.

'Beth!' I nearly jumped out of my skin when Miss Smith, our maths teacher, appeared by my desk. I looked up to meet her sharp glance.

'Finished?'

'No, Miss.'

She leant over my shoulder to look at my paper. 'You've barely started,' she said incredulously.

I twisted around nervously to meet her gaze.

'Better get a move on, the time's nearly up,' she said in her high, rasping voice, checking her watch.

As the class sank back into silence I tried to concentrate.

When Miss Smith called out 'Time's up' I handed in my test and scuttled out the door.

She called me back. 'I'd like a word with you, Elizabeth,' she said.

I only ever got my full title when I was in trouble.

'You're not making any effort with your work,' she said.

'Sorry, Miss.' I studied my shoes.

'It's not as if you can't keep up, you're a clever girl, very capable.' Her sharp, puzzled eyes bored into mine. 'If you have personal problems . . . I'd like to help.'

I hung my head, not knowing what to say.

'You could at least pay me the courtesy of looking at me when I'm speaking to you.'

'Sorry, Miss!' I looked at her, wishing I could disappear.

'Well, do you want to talk about anything?'

'No thank you, Miss.'

'Do you think that you don't have to bother, is that it?'

I stiffened. 'No, Miss.'

'Then buck up, or I'll be forced to report you to Mr Higgins.'

'Yes, Miss.'

She looked at me for a few seconds longer, then sighed. 'You may go. Treat this little chat as a warning.'

I scarpered. In the playground Goofer, Spider, Sarah and Kim were huddled together so deep in conversation that they didn't notice me approaching.

'It was all over Beth,' Goofer said.

Spider said, 'How?'

'She was with Ryan down the West Pier. Alex came on the scene. He gave Ryan a right going over,' Goofer told them.

'But she couldn't have been, she hates Ryan,' Sarah said, puzzled.

Taking a deep breath I confronted them. 'I wasn't *with* Ryan as you put it.'

Goofer turned to me. 'That gypsy beat Ryan up. He needn't think he'll get away with it.'

'Too right,' said Spider. 'We can't have him attacking us.'

'If he knows what's good for him he'll be gone before Ryan's back on his feet.'

'You're full of threats but you won't frighten Alex,' I said, sounding braver than I felt.

'We'll have to use a bit of persuasion then, won't we?' Goofer laughed. 'He'll be glad to go by the time we're finished with him.'

'That's if he can walk,' Spider said.

'Ha ha,' they laughed.

In the uncomfortable silence that followed I stood looking from one to the other.

Sarah and Kim weren't exactly supportive either. Sarah said, sanctimoniously, 'I did warn you that Alex was trouble. You should keep away from him.'

'Oh yeah!' I walked away fighting back the tears, wondering what to do. What must Alex be feeling as he waited for the fallout, I wondered, dreading the thought of it.

That evening at dinner Dad eyed me as he said, 'Ryan was in Casualty last night having his arm reset. There was a fight. Alex is supposed to have attacked him. Do you know anything about it?'

I went weak at the knees but my expression remained blank.

Dad raised his eyebrows in a query. 'No? Strange, because it's the talk of the town. Rumour has it that it was over you.'

I said, 'Yes, well, Ryan had a go at me for being friendly with Alex, then he and Alex had a fight.' I kept my voice light, knowing that there'd be hell to pay if I told the full story.

'That wasn't very clever of Alex,' said Dad. 'He could be in serious trouble if Ryan's dad decides to take it further.' He looked angry as he said, 'You stay away from both of them. Don't go near that Refugee Centre.'

'I hate Ryan Godfrey, I really hate him,' I said.

'Don't say that,' Mum said, coming into the room. 'Nobody's all bad, you know.'

Mum knew I was upset. She fussed over me, trying to make me eat my dinner. I ate a little to please her. When Dad went out I sat in a trance in front of the television, not daring to go out. Trudy looked at me mournfully. When I didn't respond she came and put her two front paws up on my lap, sensing that something was wrong.

I didn't see Alex in school the next day either – or for the rest of the week.

The following Saturday, Sarah and I went to McDonald's. It was rush hour. We queued up for cheeseburgers and chips, and sat down to eat.

Ryan, wearing shades, his arm in a sling, snaked his head round the door gauging the queue, Goofer in his wake.

'Over here,' Sarah called to them, pointing to the empty table next to us before I could stop her.

Ryan stared at me, his face expressionless, like I was some kind of pond life. When he came and sat down I turned sideways to avoid his eyes. Sarah sat so close to him that their arms were touching.

'Are you feeling better?' she asked with concern.

'Not bad, considering I could have been killed,' he said, looking at me accusingly.

All my rage surfaced. A bitter taste filled my mouth.

'Stop trying to make out it was all Alex's fault when we both know different. You asked for it,' I spat at him.

'You really think you're someone special, don't you, Beth Corrigan.' Ryan snapped, then he smirked, 'And I hear lover boy is leaving, taking off. I told you he was a coward.'

Before he could finish I bolted, knocking my food to the floor.

'Beth, wait!' Sarah called after me, but I didn't stop.

I ran all the way to the Refugee Centre to find Alex. When I got there, out of breath and panicked, he was packing all his possessions in a big hold-all.

'You're going away?' I said. 'What about school?'

'I'm not going back.'

'But you have to. There's *West Side Story* and everything.'

He shook his head. 'I tried, Beth, I really did, but it hasn't worked out. I'm not part of things here. You know that.'

'That's not true, you are,' I said, trying not to cry.

He shook his head. 'I knew there'd be problems, but I never thought that I'd be made such a scapegoat. I get blamed for everything, even the graffiti on the walls in school. It's making life difficult for me. I'm not wanted around here, Beth.'

'Where are you going to go?' I said helplessly.

'To Dublin. I know people there.'

'What about me?'

'I'll keep in touch,' he promised.

We stood looking at one another.

'I'll come with you,' I said desperately.

'You can't. Your parents would go mad. They'd come searching for you. I need to get away, Beth.'

'From me too?'

A tense silence followed. I glanced at Alex. He looked older suddenly. He saw my expression. 'There are things I have to do.'

He put his arms around me. 'Beth,' he said into my ear. 'You have to let me go.'

'But . . .' I protested.

'You'll be okay. This is your home.' He stroked my hair.

'But what about us?'

He looked down at me. 'You're better off without me. There's been nothing but trouble since I came here.'

'But you haven't done anything wrong!'

'Try telling that to the authorities – Ryan's dad is one of the heads. What chance have I got against all of them?'

'I'll tell them what happened, that you were defending me.'

'No! Don't do that. It would drag your family into it and cause even more trouble, and your Mum doesn't need that at the moment.'

'I know, but I don't want you to go.' I was crying

without even realizing it. 'I need you, Alex.' The words were out before I knew that I'd said them.

Stunned, his head snapped up in surprise. A puzzled look flashed over his face. I thought for a minute that he was going to laugh, but he didn't. Mortified, I wanted to take the last bit back. Tell him that no, I hadn't meant it, and that I'd got carried away. But the words wouldn't come out. I drew away from him in the silence that followed.

'You'll be better off without me,' he said again finally.

'You're wrong.' I sounded pathetic, but I couldn't help it.

He put his arms around me again. We stayed like that with our arms wrapped around each other and I didn't want to let go. But finally Alex broke away and picked up his bag from the floor. He kissed me on the cheek.

'I'll phone you,' he said. 'I promise.'

21

Alex didn't phone me. Each time I tried his mobile it was switched off. Every evening I went to the Refugee Centre for news of him. They had no forwarding address. Gradually, the patient expressions on the faces of the people I spoke to changed to blank stares, and I would return home aware that I was becoming a nuisance.

This was the most painful time of all, watching, waiting, with no way of knowing where he was or what was happening to him. I would pace the sea-front with Trudy hoping he would appear out of nowhere. Sometimes I would stand and peer worriedly into the motionless sea, or gaze up at the sky wondering where he was and if I'd ever see him again. I couldn't eat, or sleep, couldn't concentrate on my studies.

I wanted to talk to Becky but she was engrossed in her own life with Simon and rarely at home. I couldn't bring myself to talk to Mum about him. I didn't want to upset her.

In my diary I wrote, '*I miss him more than I ever imagined possible.*'

Two days later the doorbell rang. It was Sergeant Byrne.

'It's about Alexandru,' he said, coming straight to the point. Mum had brought him into the kitchen, where I was reading.

'Has something awful happened to him? Is he hurt?' I asked, scared.

'Do you know where he is, Beth?'

'No,' I said honestly.

'What's happened?' Mum asked.

'Jim Godfrey is pressing charges for assault on his son. It looks as though Alexandru was expecting trouble and he's scarpered. Disappearing like this really isn't in his best interest.' Sergeant Byrne gave me a doubtful look. 'You have no idea where he is?'

'No.'

It was obvious that he didn't believe me.

'The thing is, Beth, we're worried about him. Anything might happen to a young lad on his own – especially if he has gone to the city as we suspect he may have,' Sergeant Byrne said gravely.

'He could have left the country, and I wouldn't blame him if he had,' I said.

Sergeant Byrne shook his head. He put his notebook back in his pocket and picked up his jacket from the chair.

'Let me know if you hear from him,' he said, and left.

★　★　★

That night I dreamt that I went searching for Alex and found him sleeping rough, in a cardboard box under the Halfpenny Bridge. In the dream I tried to get to him but something or someone kept pulling me back. I woke up crying; I knew he was fond of me but there was a locked-up part of him that meant I couldn't get close. Still, I couldn't forget him; I just wanted to know he was safe.

When Dad heard that Jim Godfrey was going legal he was furious.

'Alex will need somebody on his side, poor lad. I'll get Derek Swan. He's the best in the business.'

'You'd do that for Alex, Dad?'

'Jim Godfrey can be a ruthless man. I'd like to see Alex get fair treatment.'

'Derek Swan costs a fortune,' Mum said, hearing this exchange.

'Let me worry about that. Now all we have to do is find Alex and tell him to stop playing silly beggars and come back to Dun Laoghaire and face the music.'

'But where to search?' said Mum.

I was sure he was in Dublin but I said nothing.

'I'll get Simon on to it, he'll know what to do,' Becky offered helpfully when she heard.

In school, *West Side Story* was put on hold. Everyone was disappointed but Potty promised its revival on Alex's return. Ryan and the gang went around with smug faces. Goofer bared his teeth every time he saw me. They were taunting me with greater effort, but I managed to ignore them: reacting would only make things worse.

As time passed and I still hadn't heard from Alex, I got really worried. I walked alone in the evenings with Trudy, keeping to the sea-front, but all hope of bumping into Alex was gone. I didn't think I'd ever see him again. Alex was lost to me; nothing left but memories to haunt me.

Mum was getting very big. She moved slowly and awkwardly and she was uncomfortable. Her life wasn't her own any more. I fetched books from the library, brought her cups of tea, and delivered daily news bulletins. She spent a lot of time in bed, only managing to get dressed in the evenings ready for when Dad got home. He seemed happier. There was a lightness in his step that hadn't been there in a long time. He would sit with her, talking instead of going back out. I could hardly believe the change in him. In spite of my own unhappiness I was glad for them both.

A harsh autumn had sneaked in unobtrusively. Early morning mists rolled in from the sea; white fingers of frost fretted the lawn. The mornings were dark, and damp. Mum ordered me to wear my grey gabardine coat, part of the school uniform. Tori scoffed at it. She wouldn't wear a coat like that, she said, even if she was to freeze to death.

One evening, passing the Refugee Centre, I met one

of the refugee boys, Zoran, who used to be friends with Alex.

'Still looking for Alex?' he asked.

'Yes, do you know where he is?'

He eyed me warily. 'Might do.'

'I need to get in touch with him, I have something important to tell him,' I said.

'I saw him the other night. He's staying with friends of mine, other refugees who have rented a house in the dockland. He's working part-time on the cargo ships, helping to load and unload.'

Zoran gave me the address and directions to get to it. I had to find Alex before anyone else did. Try and talk to him first. I decided to go the next Saturday. I could hardly believe I might see Alex again soon.

22

On Saturday morning I got up early and took a Dart to
Connelly station. It was a long walk through deserted
streets. In the cold, people were hurrying along, hunched
up into their coats. I made my way to the desolate
dockland, past the boats and cranes. I had never been to
this part of the city before. A disused railway ran parallel
to the street, whose derelict warehouses and factories had
been abandoned since the Seventies. All the doors were
boarded up. Who could possibly live here? I thought, yet
this was where my directions had led me. There was no
one to ask for help, so I walked on until I came to a row
of tenement houses at the end of a narrow road. I knocked
at the front door.

A big, greasy-looking man answered.

'Yes?' he said in a heavily accented voice, staring at me
blankly.

'I'm looking for a friend of mine. His name is
Alexandru.'

He pointed to a rickety staircase. 'Up there.'

I climbed three flights of dirty staircase. I passed

a woman carrying a baby on her way down. She smiled. I carried on up. At the door of Alex's room I stood trembling, suddenly not wanting to come face to face with him. I knocked. There was no answer. I tried the door. It opened. I was almost afraid to venture into the high-ceilinged room.

It was empty apart from a bed in one corner, a table and two chairs, a dirty stove, and a sink with a saucepan in it. I shut the door behind me. Through the grimy window I could see the grey sea, its heaving waves pounding against the sea wall. I was shivering. This was the coldest room I'd ever been in.

The door opened with a blast of more cold air as Alex swept into the room so suddenly and swiftly that he startled me.

'Beth!' For a moment he just stood transfixed, staring at me.

'Hi Alex!' I smiled, but it faded when he said abruptly, 'What are you doing here?'

I felt myself go weak with embarrassment. 'Looking for you.'

He put the bag of groceries he was carrying down on the table. 'How did you find me?' he said quietly.

'Your friend Zoren told me he met you.'

He stared at me as if I was a stranger. He looked different. He was thinner, his hair was longer and there were dark circles under his eyes, as if he hadn't slept for a long time.

He took a jar out of one of the grocery bags. 'Want a cup of coffee?' he asked, going to the sink to fill the kettle.

'Thanks, yes.'

Alex plugged in the kettle, then looked at me speculatively. 'Why did you come?'

'Alex, we need to talk. There's trouble with the Godfreys.'

'I know.'

I took a deep breath. 'Dad wants to help you.'

'How can he?'

'He has a friend who's a top lawyer.'

Alex laughed bitterly. 'Lawyers cost money,' he said, his back to me as he poured hot water into the mugs.

'Dad's willing to pay his fee,' I said, with a surge of courage.

He turned sharply. 'Why would your dad want to do that?'

'Because the charge against you is serious. Having a lawyer like Dad's friend would make all the difference. The fight with Ryan was to do with me, remember? Please accept our help. I feel awful. I've been trying to find you for ages. I went down to the centre loads of times looking for your address, but no one knew where you were. You didn't phone.'

'I thought it best to keep away.'

'This isn't right, you having to hide out here.'

'I'm not hiding out, I'm working.'

'At least come back and clear your name.'

'Do you think it would make any difference?'

'Yes, I know it would.'

He shook his head. 'They'd find some other way of branding me.'

I sipped the cup of coffee he handed me. 'So what about school? Potty is still hoping you'll come back. He's put rehearsals on hold.'

'I won't be coming back. I've got work here – enough to keep me going until my family get here. Then we'll get a place somewhere together.'

We looked silently at one another like strangers. I wondered what had happened to our closeness, the time we'd spent talking together. I wanted to scream at him to listen to me, beg him to come back with me, but I knew there was no point, he wouldn't listen. I felt flat and disappointed. I finished my coffee, put down my cup and got up to go.

'If you change your mind you know where to find me,' I said at the door.

'Beth! Wait!' He came towards me. 'Thanks for trying. I'm grateful.'

'You're welcome.' I shrugged, and went to go down the stairs.

'I've missed you.' His voice was different now, softer.

A shiver ran down my spine. 'Me too,' I whispered back.

He was beside me, pressing me to him. 'Don't go yet,'

he said. Without a word he led me back to his room. Everything was forgotten, the cold, the emptiness in my heart, the dingy tenement. Once he shut the door he turned to me and said, 'Come here.'

I closed my eyes and let him lead me over to the bed.

I woke with a start two hours later.

'Beth! Are you awake?' Alex whispered into my ear.

'Yes.'

I turned to him, remembering what we'd done, my heart racing. I opened my mouth to speak but he closed it with a kiss. Squashed together, I rested my head on his shoulder and snuggled into him. We lay like that for a long time listening to the outside noises – cranes loading cargo on to ships, the sea battering the wall, gulls crying – comforted by one another, not frightened any more.

Eventually Alex said, 'What are you thinking?'

'That you're part of me now. We'll face whatever comes our way together.' My voice was full of a confidence and hope I didn't fully feel.

He didn't reply, but moved away from me.

Silently he got out of bed, bent down and picked up his jeans, put them on.

'You are coming back with me, aren't you Alex?' I said, sitting up quickly.

He shook his head. 'No, there is no going back, I told you that,' he said firmly.

Shocked, I jumped off the bed. 'Then we'll go away together somewhere no one will know us, where we could be left alone.' I was babbling.

'There's no such place, Beth,' he said. 'It wouldn't work. We wouldn't survive a week if we tried to run away anywhere. Your parents would be frantic. You're under age. You have to go home.' There was anguish in his voice.

His eyes were miserable and I could see that he was angry with me for even making a suggestion like that. He was the cold Alex of earlier, the distance between us back. I tried to compose myself but all I felt was confusion and foolishness. More than anything else I wished I could turn the clock back. I had done something wrong, something stupid, and I was already paying for my mistake.

'I can't believe what we've just done,' I whispered. 'You have used me, Alex.'

'Beth, no! I'm sorry.'

The room felt freezing. I longed for Alex's arms around me, comforting me, but he had already moved away.

'I'll walk with you to the train station as soon as you're . . . ready.' He turned away from me and stood looking out of the window, waiting for me to go.

The room spun. I moved away. Tears splashed down my face. Alex stayed with his back to me, his hands clenched by his sides. I dressed quickly.

'Stop crying, Beth.'

I didn't reply. I grabbed my jacket and ran from the room, down the stairs.

'Beth! Wait!' I heard him calling, but I kept running until I got to the station. As soon as I was on the train I buried my face in my hands and cried all the way home, replaying the whole scene that had taken place in his room over and over again. It was a nightmare. What a fool I'd been. How could I have expected to hold him?

'What happened to you?' Dad asked, striding into the hall as soon as I opened the front door. 'We tried to get you on your mobile. Where were you?'

'I went to look for Alex.'

'Did you find him?'

'No.'

I went to walk past him. 'Don't you ever go off like that again without letting us know where you are.' He said angrily. 'You've upset your mother, and in her condition too.'

'Sorry, Dad,' I said, my hands trembling.

In bed that night I thought of Alex. I didn't really believe that I would ever see him again. I imagined him walking the streets of England all alone searching for his family, perhaps sleeping rough. I wrote in my diary, '*When he warned me off I should have listened to him.*'

I woke up in the middle of the night, numb with a dull ache around my heart like a heavy blanket. I thought of what we had done together. I had no one to talk to about it. I felt completely lost.

23

In school on Monday Tori watched me closely. 'You okay?' she asked at break.

'Yeah, why shouldn't I be?' I snapped.

She gave me a funny look. 'You're very pale. Are you sick?'

'No.'

'Want to talk about it?'

'Later.'

At lunchtime I told her what had happened, relieved to confide in someone.

She was giving me a strange look. 'You did take precautions, didn't you?'

'No.'

'Oh Beth, you can be such a fool sometimes. You could be pregnant!'

I looked at her. 'We didn't know it was going to happen.'

'That's no excuse.'

'Anyway, my period's due in the next few days . . .'

'That doesn't make any difference, you could still

have got pregnant,' she warned.

When my period didn't come I panicked.

'Get a pregnancy test kit just to be on the safe side,' Tori advised.

'I'm not pregnant,' I snapped at her. It's all this stress that's delaying it.'

'At least if you do the test you'll know for sure.'

At home I examined my body. I pulled off my top, stared at my reflection in the mirror. Nothing had changed. My stomach was flat, my breasts slightly bigger – that was due to my period coming, wasn't it? But my face was blotchy and I felt sick. I locked my door, leant against it. For the first time in ages I prayed to God to get me through this.

I lay on my bed to try to think rationally. What if I was pregnant? If I was having Alex's baby I'd have to tell him. Hope poured through me only to be dashed away again. Alex wouldn't want to know. He wouldn't want to have anything to do with me. I could never let him know. Mum and Dad would go bananas. Imagine Mum and me pregnant at the same time.

I couldn't sleep. I couldn't eat. I thought of nothing else but this new horror that confronted me. Next morning I skipped school and got the bus to Blackrock to buy a pregnancy test kit in a pharmacy where none of the assistants knew me. The bus was packed with commuters. To my shock and surprise Elvie was already on it.

'Where are you going?' she asked, her direct gaze making it difficult for me to think up something quickly.

'I have to do a message for Mum,' I said, ashamed of the lie and my real errand.

Elvie seemed to swallow it. 'I'm going to Blackrock shopping centre. I have to meet my sister-in-law and I'm late,' she said, looking at her watch.

'See you,' I called to Elvie as I got off and walked quickly to the shops. In the chemist's I felt as if the girl behind the counter was smirking as she got the kit for me. I was convinced she was about to say something. She didn't. She just wrapped it up and took my money.

Light-headed, I got the bus back to school, my heart pounding all the way. In the loo I read the instructions carefully, did the test, and waited. Sick with worry, my head spinning, I kept my eyes closed, afraid to look. When I opened them I could see the colour of the stick hadn't changed. There was no blue line. I wasn't pregnant. Almost crying with relief, I rushed to find Tori to tell her, hoping she hadn't dropped me in it with any of the teachers.

Racing down the corridor I collided with Potty.

'It's forbidden to run,' he reminded me.

'Sorry, Sir,' I panted. 'I'm late for class.'

'Why?'

'My mum was sick, Sir.'

He walked on.

Tori was as happy at the news as I was. 'Next time use a condom,' she warned.

'There won't be a next time. I'll never see Alex again.' After that first rush of relief I felt hollow inside, as if an invisible thief has snatched my baby from my stomach and made off with it, severing all hope of any connection with Alex.

I wrote in my diary, '*He is gone for good.*'

Mum was bigger than ever, blown up like a balloon. She was sentenced to bed for the rest of her pregnancy. It went against her temperament, yet she did it because she knew this was serious business, and that she'd no alternative. Dad assured us all that there was nothing to worry about. Sometimes she'd get dressed and sit at her bedroom window and watch for Dad's car.

Elvie struggled on like a martyr, doing all Mum's tasks. She was enjoying being indispensable, and was becoming bossy, ordering Becky and me about while we rushed around helping her. Mum got a bad pain in her stomach one evening.

'What's wrong?' Dad looked anxiously at her.

'Don't look so scared, it's just a bit of discomfort,' she said, white as a sheet and doubled over. 'I'll be all right, honestly. Probably the baby kicking.'

He examined her. 'I think you should let me take

you to the hospital, just to be on the safe side,' he said.

She refused to go. 'I don't want to be lounging in there for days.'

He went to make tea.

'Are you scared?' I asked her.

'No, of course not,' she said robustly, but she didn't sound convincing. 'It's nothing, your dad's fussing too much.'

'You can't be careful enough,' he said, handing her a cup of tea.

'I'm not going into hospital yet and that's that.'

Next morning Elvie tried to be helpful. 'You may need a Caesarean section,' she said. 'But that happens all the time now, right?'

Mum looked at Dad, her eyes brimming with tears. 'I'm not having them cutting me up,' she said indignantly.

Dad took her in his arms. 'Who's the doctor around here?' He glowered at Elvie as if he was fit to throttle her, and she scuttled out of the kitchen.

'Elvie and her silly ideas,' Dad said.

In drama Potty said, 'It looks as if we've lost Alexandru. We can't wait for him much longer.'

My heart went down to my boots when Ryan offered to take the part of Tony, and Potty agreed, but his heart wasn't in it since Alex had gone. Ryan went off bragging about it all over the school, of course. I loathed him more than ever.

* ★ ★

Scott phoned. He invited me to a party.

'You might enjoy it . . .' Mum encouraged me.

I decided to go. It couldn't do any harm. I made an effort to dress up, too. I wore my black cut-offs, a new black top and very high heels.

'Wow!' Scott whistled when I opened the door to him. 'You look stunning.'

'Thanks,' I said. 'I'll just get my jacket.'

We were about to leave, when Dad appeared behind me.

'Take good care of her,' he said to Scott.

'I'm not a baby, Dad,' I said, embarrassed.

'I will, Doctor Corrigan.' Scott smiled at me. 'Of course.'

The party was big, and full of noise and people I didn't know. Scott took my hand and led me to a room where people were laughing and trying to hold conversations above the blare of the music. He introduced me to his new college friends; energetic and lively boys, who all talked at once, asking questions they didn't particularly want answers to. Still, I felt grown up and it was good to laugh again.

Then Scott took my arm. 'Come on, let's go and look at the garden,' he said.

My heel got stuck in the cobblestones of the patio as we walked outside. Scott led me to a seat from which we surveyed the rolling gardens, and the cold, white moon suspended over the dark, still water below, our elbows touching. It was beautiful, but I didn't feel at ease. Scott put an arm around my shoulders. The glow of the lights from the house was on his face. His hair was ruffled. He looked handsome and anxious all at once as he said, 'What are you thinking?'

'I'm thinking what a beautiful night it is.' The truth was that I was wishing desperately that I was with Alex and not Scott.

Scott moved closer, and kissed me. It was a tender kiss but my heart wasn't in it and I moved back.

'What's the matter?' He looked hurt.

When I didn't answer he said, 'Is it to do with Alex?'

As soon as he said the name I saw Alex's face, his dark eyes, the creases around them when he smiled. I shivered.

'Cold?'

'A little.' How could I tell him that I didn't feel anything for him without upsetting him?

'I like you, Beth.'

'And I like you.'

He looked wistfully at me, his eyes shining with apprehension. 'I sense there's a "but" in there somewhere?'

'Let's just enjoy the party,' I said with an encouraging smile.

'You're right.' He took my hand. 'Let's go inside. You're frozen,' he said.

After we'd eaten something we danced, then Scott

took me home. Outside my house he kissed me on the cheek.

'It was a great party, thanks Scott.'

'Glad you enjoyed it.' He turned to me and for a second I thought he was going to kiss me again; instead he took my hand and held it.

'It's Alex you're in love with, isn't it?'

The shock of hearing him say it jolted me.

'And there's nothing I can do about it,' he added.

'I'm sorry if I hurt you, Scott.'

'Don't worry about me,' he said. 'One day you'll realize what you've missed.'

'You're probably right.' I looked at him, wishing I was older, wishing I were more sophisticated like his college friends: girls with confidence, who knew it all, knew how to handle difficult situations. I hated this bit – the growing up bit.

'I'll text you,' he said, but I knew he wouldn't.

The following Saturday morning Mum started having contractions.

'It's too early, I'm only about seven months pregnant,' she protested.

'We're going to the hospital to try and get them under control,' said Dad.

But as Mum got dressed a sharp pain tore through her. She screamed for Dad who took over, shutting us out of their bedroom. When they came downstairs Mum was shaking, though she tried to act normal. Beads of perspiration stood out on her forehead. She said goodbye to us, pretending that she wasn't too concerned, but we knew different. Dad helped her into the car, putting her bag full of night clothes and things for the baby in the boot.

She grasped Becky and me to her and whispered, 'I love you, darlings. Say a prayer. See you soon.'

Dad drove off, Mum looking tearful in the back seat.

Back inside Elvie sang loudly to keep us cheerful but I wasn't fooled. She was as anxious as we were. I tried to be adult and calm, but I couldn't help thinking of what Mum was going through. I feared for the baby, too. It was coming far too soon. Elvie made tea and sat me down.

'Don't worry, Beth, they'll do something to stop the contractions and when it's ready the baby'll slip out easily, not a bother.' She seemed to know everything there was to know about babies.

'Yes – don't fret. Mum's as tough as old boots,' said Becky, joining us.

I looked at Becky wishing I were as calm as she was. I couldn't relax so I ate my way through a bowl of cereal and a packet of crisps, watching my box-set of *Buffy* for hours.

'Where's your mum?' Tori demanded when she called for me later for a hockey match.

I told her and made her swear not to tell Granny and Grandad, so as not to worry them.

'Okay,' she agreed. 'Is your mum going to be all right?'

'I hope so. Unless something goes wrong?' I said anxiously.

Tori's arm was around me. 'Look, she'll be fine,' she said, though knowing as little about it as I did.

But Mum was back home at tea-time. She was hunched up on the sofa. Dad was making tea.

'False alarm, thank God,' she said, before I got a word out.

'Oh Mum!' I went to her, held her tight.

'It's good for the baby to have as much time in the womb as possible,' she said. 'So they told me, anyway.'

'Stop worrying,' Dad said to me later. 'We're all here for her, she'll have the best care and attention when the time comes. She's got the best obstetrician in the country looking after her.'

24

Even though Mum was back on an even keel, I was still going to bed each night exhausted, unable to sleep thinking of Alex. I wondered where he was and what he was doing. The worst thing was the guilt I felt about my part in it all. It was because of me that Alex had gone — and now he was in big trouble.

Finally, tired of my secret, I confided in Granny, sitting in her kitchen savouring the wonderful, comforting smell of her cooking. I told her how Alex had saved me from Ryan's attack, coming on the scene just in time, and how it was that incident that had led to the fight between him and Ryan that had caused him to leave Dun Laoghaire. Shocked, Granny finally said, 'You should have reported this, Beth!'

'I couldn't. Dad would have gone ballistic and Mum, in her condition . . .'

'You should have come to me, then.'

'I know and I'm sorry I didn't.

She listened in silence while I told her how anxious I was about Alex and how much I missed him. I went as far as telling her that I thought I was in love with him.

She didn't laugh at me. 'I was in love with your grandad at your age,' she said. 'And when he went off to England I thought that he didn't care about me and that I'd never see him again.'

'What happened?' I asked eagerly.

'He came home for a short while, then dropped the bombshell that he was joining the British Army. Then I did think he was gone out of my life for good. But I didn't lose hope. I didn't give up on him.'

'What did you do?'

'I kept writing to him, and eventually I went over to spend a holiday with him.' Her eyes twinkled as she said, 'That did the trick.'

'So what do you think I should do?' I asked her eagerly.

'The city's not a safe place these days for a boy on his own.'

'He won't come back.'

She was thoughtful as she said, 'Can't you try and persuade him to come back? He's welcome to stay here. There's plenty of room. He can have the basement to himself if he wants privacy. The bedroom is bright and airy, and I could fix it up for him.'

'Oh Granny, that's a brilliant idea. But what would Grandad say? Would he mind?'

'Of course not, he's very fond of Alex. Tell you what, we'll go and see Alex, and talk him into coming home.

Now let's have dinner. Tori!' she called up the stairs. 'Dinner's ready.' To me she said with glee, 'She likes my Cajun chicken.'

'What'll she have to say about Alex moving in?' I asked, anxiously.

'She wants to move in with you. I'll have to talk to your dad about it.'

'It won't be a problem,' I said. 'She's round our house most of the time anyway.'

It was rush hour in the city, bars and restaurants were full, their lights reflected on the wet streets, and their cooking smells blending with the traffic fumes. We took a taxi to the tenement house in the dockland, and knocked on the door. The man I'd seen the last time let us in. We went up the stairs, Granny clutching the banisters, me trying to stay calm as I knocked on his door. There was no answer. We heard the front door slam, and footsteps in the hall. Alex came running up the stairs. When he got to the landing he stared at us in amazement.

'Beth! Mrs Scanlon!'

'Hello Alex,' Granny said.

He was pale, his eyes were hollow, and his cheeks had caved in.

'You've lost weight, Alex,' Granny said.

He pushed his damp hair out of his eyes. 'It's the work. All hours.' He opened the door of his room to let us in.

'Alex, I won't beat about the bush,' said Granny. 'I want you to come home.'

He frowned. 'Home?'

'Mr Scanlon and I would like you to come and stay with us. We don't like the thought of you living alone in the city, we think that it would be a good idea if you came back to Dun Laoghaire.'

'I couldn't possibly do that,' said Alex.

'It'd be nice to have a strong young man around the place to give us a hand with the chores. It's a big house and we're not getting any younger. Besides, we owe you a great debt of gratitude for saving Beth from a most horrific experience.'

Alex turned to me. 'You told her?'

'I had to,' I said.

Granny said, 'If you hadn't been there that night God knows what might have happened.' Her voice broke.

'Ryan's got your part in *West Side Story* and he's useless,' I said.

There was a hint of a smile on Alex's face as he said, 'You've got it all worked out, haven't you?'

Granny gave him a look. 'You can't let Ryan get away with this. He can't be allowed to get away with attempted rape. He'll strike again, probably succeed the next time. Have you thought of that?'

Wearily, Alex nodded his head. 'I've thought about nothing else.'

'This is important, Alex. The Gardai are involved, you're under investigation, which means they want to talk to you.'

Alex threw up his hands. 'What's the point in going back? I haven't got a hope against Ryan Godfrey, and his big-shot dad.' He turned away in frustration. 'I don't want all that trouble again.'

'The law is a complicated process, Alex. We have to get you a lawyer. There's a lot to sort out. The Guards will be interested in hearing what you have to say. Beth will be interviewed too. She'll have to tell her side of the story. There'll be charges against Ryan for assault, and attempted rape.'

Alex was silent, reflective.

Granny continued, 'And what about your education? There's school to think of. You're clever, you've got a bright future ahead of you — if you stick with your studies.'

Alex looked uncertain as he said, 'I've missed a lot.'

'You'll catch up. We'll go and leave you to think about it. We care what happens to you,' Granny said.

He raised his hand. 'Thank you. Thanks for the offer. It means a lot to me.'

'We'll give you time to think about it,' Granny said.

Alex bit his lip. 'I need to find my family. Otherwise, I'll have no one belonging to me. No one of my own flesh and blood.'

'We'll help you with that, too,' Granny said. 'Beth, phone the taxi rank.'

Outside the wind whipped my hair around my face. Alex smoothed it back behind my ears.

'Bye Beth,' he said. 'Bye Mrs Scanlon, thanks for everything.'

She shook hands with him. 'You're welcome,' she said. 'Think about what I said, and don't forget we're on your side.'

'I will. I'll phone you, let you know what's happening.' His eyes were on me.

'Promise me,' I said.

'I promise.'

On the way to the station Granny said, 'I'll give him a key to the basement door, he can come and go as he pleases.' She paused and smiled at me. 'Yes, that's what I'll do.'

25

The following Saturday afternoon I was at Granny's, playing the piano. To be honest I was just striking the notes, my heart not in it, when I heard the doorbell and voices in the hall. Then the sitting-room door opened. Alex was standing there.

My heart jolted. I could tell from his eyes that his did too.

'Alex!' I jumped to my feet, tears of relief at seeing him again stinging my eyes. 'I thought you might have decided not to come,' I said, trembling. 'You didn't phone.'

'I know, your Granny told me. My mobile was stolen. Anyway, here I am.' His eyes burned into mine.

I could feel my heart beating . . .

Granny stepped into the room. 'We got your bedroom ready for you. Go and have a look while I make you something to eat.'

'I don't want to be any trouble.'

'You won't be,' she assured him.

'Like it?' I asked when we got downstairs.

'It's great.' Alex paced around the large bedroom taking in the dark furniture, the big old-fashioned bed.

'And you have it all to yourself. It's nice and private down here.'

'It's smashing. I really appreciate this, Beth.'

Being alone with him was difficult; something I hadn't expected. I felt both ecstatic that he was back and annoyed that he had put me through so much worry.

'You can be all on your own here,' I said eventually.

He leaned towards me. 'I won't want to be on my own all of the time . . .'

His words trailed off as Granny's voice called down to us that tea was ready.

'Why don't you go down to The Deep End to see about getting your job back?' Grandad suggested later.

After tea we went down to The Deep End to see Jim, the manager. He was delighted to see Alex and only too pleased to have him back. Alex and I decided to walk back via the pier, which was the worst thing we could have done. We'd only walked a few yards when we ran straight into Ryan and the boys.

Ryan's head snapped up in amazement. He stared at Alex wide-eyed.

'What's he doing here?' he said. He stepped forward, Goofer and Spider close behind him. 'I thought you'd gone.'

Alex was calm. 'Well, now I'm back,' he said, taking

hold of my arm and trying to move past Ryan.

Ryan's face tightened.

'I don't want to play any more games with you, Ryan,' said Alex. 'Can you let me pass, please?'

Ryan's face puckered into a grin. 'Games! This isn't a game. You tried to kill me.'

'Don't exaggerate,' Alex said, in a detached way.

Ryan's teeth were clenched, as if he were reining in some kind of violence, but before he could act, Alex slipped past them, down the path. Ryan and Goofer lunged after him. Ryan jumped on Alex and pinned him to the ground.

Alex struggled, got a grip on Ryan, and lifted him off the ground. For a split second they teetered on the edge, then Ryan fell into the sea. There was a screeching cry and flap of wings as seagulls rose up, angry at being disturbed. Then a terrible silence as Alex looked around wildly for a moment, then slipped down after him, his feet scrabbling madly as he slithered on the rocks. Goofer followed.

Ryan was lying face down. Goofer got his hands under Ryan's head and lifted it up. There was a deep, bloody gash on his forehead where he'd bashed it on the rocks. Panting frantically, Alex and Goofer raised him up on to the rocks. Ryan's head lolled. He stirred, and his eyes opened momentarily, but he seemed unable to focus properly.

'He's passing out,' Goofer shouted.

'Ring for an ambulance!' Alex shouted.

Shaking all over, I took out my mobile and dialled 999.

I reported an accident, giving the location, praying Ryan wouldn't die before the ambulance arrived. Then I phoned Dad and told him what happened, adding, 'Get here quick.'

'Don't move him, I'm on my way,' he said.

Goofer said to Alex, 'You'd better not try and sneak off, I'm going to get you for this.' He said it mildly but his face had a fierce expression on it.

In the fading light the gash on the side of Ryan's head looked worse. It was swelling up. His eyes were dark sockets in his white face.

Dad arrived within minutes.

'It was an accident, he slipped,' I said, too quickly.

Dad examined Ryan and kept vigil over him until the ambulance came, its siren wailing. I watched as the paramedics lifted Ryan carefully into the ambulance. He looked dead.

As the paramedics drove away Goofer turned on Alex. 'If he dies you're a murderer.'

It was all starting again. Alex might be in real trouble this time, too – even though it was not his fault. I was sure of that. But I was scared, too.

Dad drove us home. I felt cold and numb with the shock of what had happened and Alex didn't say a word. He just sat with his face turned to the window. When we arrived home, Dad made us tea, but he wasn't staying.

'Try to get some sleep. I'm going back to the hospital,' he told us.

Alex drank his tea, but then, giving me a brief hug, he went over to Granny's to tell her the news.

Upstairs, Mum was in bed. Becky was waiting up for me in her room.

'Beth! What's happened now?'

'He's such a show-off that Ryan,' I told her tearfully. 'I shouted for them to stop and they didn't take any notice. I'm scared, Becky, really scared.'

I burst into tears.

She came to me, put her arms around me. 'Tell me,' she said.

It all came pouring out. I told her everything; all the details about Ryan's rape attempt. I told her all the personal stuff about Alex and me, even about the pregnancy scare, my heart breaking.

She listened intently then said, 'God, you've been through it, haven't you? Poor thing, having all that bottled up inside you.' Her arms were tight around me.

'I didn't know who to talk to, except for Granny.' I sobbed with relief.

She looked at me closely. 'Alex is really fond of you, you know.'

'What makes you say that?'

'It's obvious,' she said matter-of-factly. 'That's why he came back.'

'How do you know?'

She squeezed my shoulders. 'I probably know everything

there is to know about boys with what Simon's put me through.'

'But it's such a disaster, Becky.' I put my head in my hands. 'Now he's got caught up with Ryan and those awful bullies again. Bringing him back here was a mistake.'

'Oh Beth, don't be stupid, of course it wasn't.'

I took a deep breath to steady myself, determined not to cry. 'How could it all have gone so wrong?'

'You've got to tell Dad what you told me about the rape attempt.'

'I can't. He'll go mad.'

'That doesn't matter. You have to do it. Don't you see, it changes everything.'

She made me a cup of tea, adding two heaped spoonfuls of sugar for shock, and fussed around me like an old mother hen.

Waiting for Dad to return was the worst part. Becky and I went downstairs to the kitchen so as not to disturb Mum. We were on our third cup of tea when Dad finally got back.

'How's Ryan?' I asked him straight away.

'He'll live, he's lucky there was no severe damage, but his father's livid. Luckily he doesn't know where Alex is living or he'd be round there in a flash. Get your coat on, Beth, we're going to Granny's. We have to see Alex, sort this business out.'

'Now?'

'Right now, it's important.'

At Granny's, Dad took Alex and me into the sitting-room and shut the door.

'I want to talk seriously to you both,' he said.

White-faced, Alex looked at him but stayed quiet.

'Tell me everything that happened.'

'Ryan and Goofer attacked Alex,' I said.

'Getting their own back for the previous fight,' Alex said.

'Why did you beat Ryan up in the first place?' Dad asked.

Alex sneaked a glance at me. 'I can't tell you that, Doctor Corrigan. It would be betraying a confidence.'

Dad threw his hands up. 'You've got to tell me, otherwise I can't help you.'

'It was my fault,' I burst out. 'Ryan attacked me that night on the West Pier, he tried to rape me.'

Shocked, Dad said, 'What!'

'I was going to meet Alex at the studio,' I began, and told him the whole story, every detail, shivering, back there in the dark, feeling Ryan's dirty hands all over me again, seeing his leering eyes, his open mouth. I felt my flesh crawl. I couldn't look at Dad.

Alex said, 'I came upon the scene. I was trying to stop him – it all got out of hand.'

Dad looked at me in an admonishing way. 'Why didn't you tell me this before, Beth?'

'I was too ashamed.' I slumped down into my

chair and dropped my head in shame.

'You had nothing to be ashamed about. You should have told someone.'

I looked up at him helplessly. 'I was scared as well, that you'd go ballistic.'

Dad paced up and down. 'But don't you see this puts a whole different complexion on the story?'

'I do now.'

Dad's face was gaunt as he said, 'I knew you'd been keeping things to yourself Beth, but this is a very serious matter, and has to be dealt with. I'll phone Derek Swan in the morning. Tell him what you've just told me. He'll want to talk to you both.'

'Yes,' Alex agreed.

'Meantime, go back to school and take no notice of anything that might be said to you.'

He put his hand on Alex's shoulder, squeezed it. 'Thank you for rescuing my daughter. The consequences of rape don't bear thinking about. I owe you a debt of gratitude. You're a good lad.'

The next few days were hectic. Derek Swan listened to our dreadful stories. Dad backed us to the hilt.

Everyone was glad to see Alex back at school. Nobody mentioned what had happened. Even Goofer and Spider kept well out of his way.

Potty was over the moon at having him back in *West Side Story*, too.

'Obviously we've missed Christmas. We'll make it for Easter. We'll give three performances in the new Pavilion Theatre.'

'Wow!' We were impressed.

'Well, the old hall is out of commission.' He gave us a sidelong glance.

Potty's enthusiasm was unquenchable. 'It'll be hectic. We'll have posters all over the town, in every shop window, every bar and restaurant, and flyers to spread the word.'

Straight away we went over to rehearsals, singing our hearts out. It was a release after all the gloom and doom of the past weeks.

'This is going to be a fantastic production – really. You'll be brought to people's attention, Alexandru,' Potty told him. 'There'll be reviews in the newspapers. I have a feeling you're going to go down very well. You're showing great promise.'

Everyone went home exhilarated. Finally we had something to be excited about.

26

I woke in the middle of the night hearing footsteps, and Mum moaning. I leapt out of bed and ran into their bedroom.

Dad was helping Mum put on her dressing-gown. 'I'm taking her to the hospital,' he said.

I kissed her goodbye quickly, then Dad helped her downstairs and into the car. Becky was awake by then, too, and we watched from the window as they drove off.

'She looks terrible,' I said.

'So would you if you were about to give birth.'

I went back to bed promising God I'd do anything as long as Mum was all right. It was a long time before I finally fell asleep. My mobile rang at seven o'clock, jolting me upright. I fumbled for it. It was Dad.

'You have a baby sister,' he said. His voice was tired, but full of happiness.

'Oh Dad!' I felt my mouth go dry. 'Is Mum all right?'

'She's fine and so is the baby.' He chuckled happily into the phone. 'She's in an incubator, all wired up with tubes and stuff, but she's a fighter.'

'Oh Dad!'

'She'll be fine.' His voice was optimistic.

'When was she born?'

'Just half an hour ago. I've been with your mother ever since.'

'How is she?'

'She's resting now, she's exhausted.'

'When can I see her?'

'Later on today. I'll be home to collect you and Becky.' His laugh was one of relief.

I woke Becky up with the news. Wide awake with excitement, we went downstairs to make tea and talk.

I told Elvie as soon as she arrived in the morning. She gave a whoop of joy and danced around the kitchen, her silver sandals glittering.

That afternoon Dad took us to the hospital. I was nervous and excited as I followed him along the corridor.

Mum was asleep, propped up on her pillows. She looked as vulnerable as a small child. I wanted to hug her but I couldn't disturb her.

Dad beckoned us out into the corridor. 'Would you like to see your sister?'

She lay in an incubator, the tiniest baby I'd ever seen. She looked like a bird in a nest. Though her skin was red and there was a tube up her nose, she was perfect. She even had eyelashes.

'She's beautiful, Dad,' I whispered.

'What's the tube for?' Becky asked.

'It's to help her to breathe until she can to manage on her own.'

'When will that be?' I asked.

He smiled. 'We'll have to wait and see. She's doing fine. She's a toughie, aren't you darling?' he said into the incubator.

Mum was awake when we got back to her room.

'Mum!' I went to her, too choked up to say anything. Becky hugged her too.

'Did you see her?' she asked eagerly, her own eyes filled with tears.

'She's beautiful, Mum, really beautiful,' Becky said.

'Isn't she?' Mum said proudly. 'I wish I could hold her.' There was longing in her voice.

'You will soon, darling,' Dad consoled her, his hand holding hers.

'What are you going to call her?'

'Mia, it's a diminutive of Mary,' Mum said. 'After my sister Mary, who wasn't so fortunate.' She looked at Dad.

'Granny will be pleased,' he said.

We left the hospital just as Granny and Grandad arrived. We were walking on air. I couldn't wait to tell Tori the great news.

Later in the week Mum came home, but without Mia. She was kept in for another few days. I went to visit her each evening and could see her gaining strength. Then one afternoon when I came in from school Mum was in the kitchen with Mia clutched in her arms. She laid her in my lap, and I held her for the first time. She was light as a feather, her newborn smell mingled with the scent of baby lotion, her tiny face barely visible beneath her white bonnet.

'Hello beautiful,' I said to her.

She stared up at me, her dark blue eyes trying to focus. Her fingers plucked the air, her tiny face puckered.

'Don't cry.' I cradled her, and sang to her, '*Hush little baby don't you cry . . .*'

She snuggled into me, her body warm against mine. I wanted to hold her forever and protect her. I wanted to take her everywhere, show her off, but eventually I handed her back to Mum for her feed.

Over the next few days I went everywhere with my new sister. I pushed her pram proudly along the sea-front, Mia fast asleep, bundled up, not a care in the world. Mum walked beside me. The sea was grey; gulls whirled around the boats. The wind cut through us as we walked along, Trudy slouching on her lead. When Mum took Mia to the clinic for her check-up I insisted on going with her, on my way to meet Tori in The Rainbow Café.

'People will think she's your baby,' Mum said.

I smiled, thinking what a close call I'd had in that area.

In spite of her happiness, though, Mum was edgy. The thought of anything being wrong with Mia terrified her.

'I'm sure the clinic will be delighted with her, she's gaining weight,' I said.

'I hope so.'

At the clinic Mum said, 'I'll see you at home later.'

I kissed Mia on the forehead. 'Good luck,' I said, watching as they went inside.

On Marine Road I saw Tori coming towards me. Her hair was blowing around her face.

'It's freezing,' she said, walking quickly.

Trudy dawdled along. 'Come on, lazybones,' I said to her.

I tied her lead to the railing. 'I won't be long, I'll bring you out something nice.' She flopped down to wait in the shelter of the doorway, uninterested.

'I don't know what's wrong with Trudy, she's not the best.'

'Her nose has been put out of joint. She's not the baby in the family any more,' Tori said.

In the café Tori said, 'Mum phoned. She's got a new boyfriend.'

'Really! Who is he?'

'She didn't say much about him.'

'Did you ask her?'

She sighed. 'No, I suppose I don't want to know. Knowing about them means you have to accept them.'

'Funny attitude.'

She shrugged. 'I'll soon find out. She coming for the christening, bringing him with her.'

'Tori, that's great!'

Tori made a face. 'Is it?'

'Aren't you pleased?'

267

'No, she'll only want to drag me back to Canada and I don't want to go.'

Mum was back when I got home.

'Mia's coming along fine. They're very pleased with her.'

'I knew they would be,' I said, taking Mia and cuddling her.

She smiled a brilliant smile at me, stretched her fingers out and grasped my index finger.

'Clever girl!' I said. 'I can't wait for you to start crawling, and walking and talking.'

Mum laughed. 'Steady on, give her a chance.'

The charge of assault was dropped. The fact that Alex had used reasonable force under extreme provocation and in defence of another person was taken into consideration. Alex got off with a caution. But as a potential rapist, Ryan was facing trial.

Mia was christened in Saint Michael's Church. At two o'clock sharp, family and friends gathered at the church. It was December the twenty-second, my birthday.

Granny sat in the front row in a new blue coat and hat; Grandad was in his best dark suit. Colleen looked gorgeous in a rainbow-coloured coat, her nails painted red to match her lipstick. Beside her sat her boyfriend, Baxter, a thin man with a dickey bow and a rakish smile.

Vicky, who'd flown in the day before, was resplendent in a pale yellow coat and hat to match, and diamond earrings; she made a grand entrance. Eyes turned to look at her with admiration.

'What a great occasion this is,' Father Murphy said.

Mum was radiant in a red suit, her hair a golden halo. Mia was dressed in a long silk christening robe, flounced and ruched with lace on the neck and sleeves, which Granny's Gran had made for her firstborn and was now a family heirloom. Becky held her tightly while Dad looked on proudly as they silently waited for Father Murphy to perform the ceremony.

'I baptize you, Mia, Gabriella, Corrigan,' Father Murphy announced, pouring freezing holy water on poor Mia's tiny head.

She looked up at Becky in astonishment, then opened her mouth and bawled. Becky rocked her, panic-stricken. She looked over at Mum, who smiled reassuringly.

'She has a fine pair of lungs, thank God,' Father Murphy said.

Everyone went back to our house, the rooms filled with laughter and talking. Everyone who had been invited had turned up. There were presents for Mia, pretty dresses, a beautiful porcelain doll from Vicky, and boxes of toys in silver wrappings.

'Not footloose and fancy-free any more, then?' Grandad asked Colleen.

'I'm afraid not,' Colleen said with a grin at Baxter.

'She always had the men eating out of her hand,' said Vicky.

'Like mother like daughter,' Grandad said wryly.

'Baxter's nice,' Mum whispered.

'Very eligible, too,' Vicky emphasized. 'He owns a circus.'

Silver balloons hung from the ceiling, taut as drums. A huge 'Welcome to Baby Mia' sign swung from the chandelier over a beautifully set table, and a log fire crackled in the grate.

Dad, red-faced, proudly carved the turkey and ham. Elvie in a gold lame dress served the hot plates of food. Tori and I helped her. Alex looked after the drinks. For pudding there was sherry trifle, and Vicky's favourite, pavlova and cream, plus several flavoured ice creams, and a huge cake with 'Welcome Baby Mia' written on it.

Champagne corks popped. Vicky protested that she wanted 'just a drop', when her glass was filled to 'wet the baby's head'.

'Long legs to the baby,' Grandad said, raising his glass.

Vicky monopolized Mia, taking her in her arms and cradling her. 'She has a definite look of you around the eyes, Peter,' she declared to Grandad. He beamed with pleasure.

'They're obviously looking after you properly, Tori,' Vicky said. 'When I lived here as a child I was positively pampered.'

'You do exaggerate, Vicky,' Granny said.

'Then I always did,' Vicky said, and whispered something in Granny's ear, which made them both laugh.

The two seemed inseparable as they sat together, their childhood bond unbroken. Watching them I thought what a pity it was that they lived so far apart.

Voices filled the room, all talking at once of the old days, Grandad saying, 'We were poor but we were happy.'

Granny took umbrage. 'Anyone would think we had nothing,' she sniffed.

These reminders of long ago meant everything to them, and little to us.

'You don't have to worry about Tori any more. I'm taking her back to Toronto with me,' Colleen announced.

'I'm not going back,' Tori declared defiantly. 'I like it here.'

Vicky turned to Colleen. 'There's no need to do anything hasty. You can postpone your wedding plans, let Tori finish out the year. You don't want to undo all the good work that's been done on her. Look how much she's improved.'

'Have the wedding here,' Tori pleaded. 'I won't have to be uprooted, then you can go round the world with Baxter on your honeymoon.'

'I don't know whether Baxter will fall in with these plans. I do want to do the right thing,' Colleen said.

'That'd be a first,' Vicky said.

Tori looked at Colleen hopefully as she suggested, 'Tell

you what, I'll go home next summer, and come back in the autumn. That'll give you plenty of time to work out what you want to do.'

'I might go with you,' Scott said. 'Get a summer job over there.'

'Oh please, please do,' Tori said. 'I'm sure Mum will agree to it.'

'All right, then,' Colleen said, giving Scott a big smile. 'I'm too soft-hearted for my own good.'

The Christmas pudding was doused in brandy and lit. A blue blaze shot up into the air and the 'Welcome to Baby Mia' sign was set alight. With a loud bang it fell on to the table. Smoke billowed, the balloons burst. Pandemonium ensued.

'Fire!' shouted Elvie, waving a tea-towel frantically in the air like a cop in O'Connell Street.

'Call the fire brigade!' cried Granny.

'No need, outside at once,' bellowed Baxter.

We stumbled out into the darkness, wheezing and coughing. Baxter strutted to and forth and astounded and impressed everyone by battering his way through the thick smoke, proficiently performing acts of bravery with buckets of water, a coat thrown over his head, Trudy barking at his boots.

Water gushed out of the hall door. The neighbours gathered outside.

'The house will collapse,' sobbed Mum.

'Solid as a rock,' assured Baxter. 'Everything's under

control. Now let the party begin,' he called out, leading the way back inside to the sitting-room. There he revved up the new piano I had got for my birthday with 'Knees Up Mother Brown'.

'You're a marvel,' Granny said.

'I used to be in the circus,' Baxter boasted.

'Doing what?' she asked.

'Rope-walking, trick-cycling, juggling.'

'He'll try anything,' Colleen said.

'I'll bet,' said Tori. 'Do you walk on water too?' she asked cheekily.

'I'm willing to give it a try if it'd make you happy.' Baxter grinned.

Even Tori laughed, seeing him in a new light and liking what she saw.

'He's a charmer, all right,' praised Elvie.

Tori and Alex sang 'Maria', their voices merging beautifully. Everyone clapped. Grandad got out his guitar and sang a couple of Elvis Presley songs, strutting up and down with the guitar held aloft.

His brother Jimmy joined in. He'd come all the way from Cork with his wife, Cora, when he heard Vicky was here. He swanned around, a fat cigar in his mouth, boasting about the fleet of trucks he had in his haulage business.

'Jamming up the traffic, polluting the atmosphere,' Grandad teased him. But I could tell he was proud of his younger brother's success.

Simon left in a mood. Becky, Tori and I cleared up. Becky was quiet for once.

'Trouble?' I asked her.

Simon was furious when I said I was going to the christening without him. It's not my fault he wasn't invited.' For once she seemed eager to talk to me about him. 'He's says I don't love him enough.'

'And do you?'

'I thought I did. Oh, I don't know.'

'He'll be back tomorrow, knocking down the door,' Tori said.

Becky wasn't so sure.

Later Alex and I went for a walk. Dawdling home, we stopped at the new marina to admire the boats. It was beautiful, and peaceful, not a soul around, the sea calm, the waves washing languidly against the shore. A gentle breeze caressed my face.

'Happy Birthday, Beth!' Alex held out a tiny present wrapped in pink tissue paper and tied with a silver ribbon.

It was a pair of blue stone earrings set in silver.

'Alex! Where did you get these?'

'I made them for you at the centre,' he said proudly. 'I've had them ages.'

'They're beautiful,' I said.

He kissed me. I felt I was floating.

'Don't talk,' he said, holding me.

I didn't. I could have stayed in his arms forever. I felt we were living a fairy tale, different people to the ones who so recently had been caught up in so much trouble. Eventually he let me go.

Epilogue

It's nearly summer. It is a golden afternoon, though slightly chilly. I am sitting in my tree writing in my diary, wrapped in a rug. *West Side Story* was a great success. Alex looked gorgeous on stage. He's thinking about becoming an actor. The praise he got and good reviews have all made him think differently about his life and what he wants.

His family is living here now, too. Alex finally tracked them down through the Irish Refugee Agency, who located them in a centre in the south of England. It was a wonderful day when they arrived at Granny and Grandad's house. They all hugged and hugged each other. Alex's mother is a beautiful woman, though frail with sad eyes. I thought they would never stop crying. Alex didn't say a word at first, I don't think he could speak. His brother, Misha, is so handsome, Sarah's fallen head over heels for him; lucky for her Tori's affections are elsewhere. She and Scott are inseparable. Dad got Alex's family fixed up in a flat and they are on the housing list.

Mia is growing bigger by the day. Like Mum said, she has brought a breath of fresh air to our home. Even Trudy has accepted her and loves guarding her pram.

Ryan was given a jail sentence of three years to be reviewed regularly. He'll probably get out after eighteen months if he manages to behave himself. The fact that he was the son of a politician didn't hold any sway. We talked about it, Alex and I, quietly on our own, not bitter or angry, but chastened and changed by the whole wretched business. Alex got off with a caution, but was warned that he must never take the law into his own hands again. He should have reported the bullying early on, the family liaison officer said. Alex has learnt a lot from the experience. I look at him sometimes and can't believe how confident he has become.

I'll let you in on a secret. After the last performance of *West Side Story*, Alex told me he loved me. I asked him in a shaky voice if he could repeat it, slowly, unable to believe that he had said those words. He did, and when I looked at him I knew it was true. I told him I loved him too.

The sun's gone in, it's getting cold. I write, '*For a long time I feared that having been hurt so much by Ryan and the boys might put Alex off living here, but everything is working out right.*' My fingers are numb as I write, '*I love you Alex,*' to the end of the page.

That's my story for now. The summer's coming soon. Life is good.